Praise for Colin Mochrie and *Not Quite the Classics*

"*Not Quite the Classics* ... is Mochrie doing what he does best: riffing off a theme with a unique comic vision."
— *Toronto Star*

"Colin Mochrie is a comedic and creative force to be reckoned with. Therefore, this book is a literary force to be reckoned with. If you are too lazy for reckoning, just read this book and everything will work out nicely."
— Brad Sherwood

"Colin Mochrie is devastatingly handsome, perilously smart, and smells like warm maple syrup. Step inside his hilarious and complex mind, and abandon all hope."
— Aisha Tyler

"I adore Colin Mochrie. I think he is brilliant, so talented, and a dear, sweet man. Also, he's funny as hell and a good kisser!"
— Florence Henderson

"Colin's greatest attributes are his unique sense of humour, his kindness to his fellow man, and his uncanny ability to retain everything I've taught him the last thirty years."
— Ryan Stiles

"I love Colin. I love his voice. I love his lips. I love his eyeballs. His pecs. And the rest of him. I'm going to Paris with him soon."
— Richard Simmons

PENGUIN

NOT QUITE THE CLASSICS

COLIN MOCHRIE was born in Scotland and grew
up in Canada. He is best known for his roles
on *Whose Line Is It Anyway?* and *This Hour Has
22 Minutes*. He was influenced by the writings
of Charles Dickens, Dr. Seuss, and Stephen King,
and fulfilled his lifelong ambition to write a book
after his agent forced him into it. Mochrie lives
in Toronto with his wife, Debra.

Colin Mochrie

Not QUITE the Classics

PENGUIN
an imprint of Penguin Canada,
a division of Penguin Random House Canada Limited

Penguin Canada, 320 Front Street West, Suite 1400,
Toronto, Ontario, M5V 3B6, Canada

First published in Viking hardcover by Penguin Canada, 2012
Published in this edition, 2014

2 3 4 5 6 7 8 9 10

Copyright © Colin Mochrie, 2012
Photographs copyright © by Aaron Cobb, 2012

"Re:Becker" reproduced with permission of Curtis Brown Group Ltd, London on behalf of
The Chichester Parnership. Copyright © Daphne Du Maurier 1938.

All rights reserved. Without limiting the rights under copyright reserved above, no part
of this publication may be reproduced, stored in or introduced into a retrieval system, or
transmitted in any form or by any means (electronic, mechanical, photocopying, recording
or otherwise), without the prior written permission of both the copyright owner and the
above publisher of this book.

*Publisher's note: This book is a work of fiction. Names, characters, places, and incidents either
are the product of the author's imagination or are used fictitiously, and any resemblance to
actual persons living or dead, events, or locales is entirely coincidental.*

Printed and bound in the United States of America

Library and Archives Canada Cataloguing in Publication

Mochrie, Colin, 1957–, author
Not quite the classics / Colin Mochrie.

Short stories.
Reprint: Originally published: Toronto : Viking, c2012.
ISBN 978-0-14-318383-9 (pbk.)

I. Title.

PS8626.O34N67 2014   C813'.6   C2014-904435-6

www.penguinrandomhouse.ca

Penguin
Random House
PENGUIN CANADA

To Deb and Kinley
For making life easier than it's supposed to be

Introduction

Writing is a lot of work, and as it happens, I am not a fan of work. One of the reasons I became an improviser was so that my workload would be light. I don't have to learn lines or go for wardrobe fittings. I don't have to travel with equipment or an entourage (mainly because no one wants to do things for me). I just need a stage, and someone to work with, and off I go. Simple. Easy. No heavy lifting. The best thing about writing is that I am sitting down while I do it. The worst thing, and I cannot stress this enough, is that it is work.

If you were to transcribe any of the scenes we did on *Whose Line is it Anyway?*, they would rarely, if ever, make sense. Each scene was a mixture of suggestions from the audience, our own creativity, and sometimes, liquor. Improvisation is an art form of the moment, and each moment can lead to a multitude of tangents that for that brief time make absolute sense. Writing a book, though, means making sense *forever*. That's work. And don't get me started on punctuation and spelling ... (Those three little dots that lead to nowhere? It's called an ellipsis. Who knew? Who needs to know?)

I never wanted to write a book. (Period.)

Don't get me wrong. I love books. From the very first classic I read—*The Cat in the Hat*—I was hooked. Books made up the bulk of my birthday and Christmas presents. Then I discovered the public library. Having been blessed with the ability to read quickly, and early, I'd take out seven books every week, finish them, then head back for more. Every genre intrigued me. Louis L'Amour westerns, Isaac Asimov's *Foundation Trilogy*, Dashiell Hammett's crime novels, *Peanuts* and *Doonesbury* comic-strip collections. Books taught me everything from how to stickhandle a puck and build models to how to cook dinner, mix a cocktail, and find a cheap hotel in Paris. Books were invaluable to me during the raging hormones of puberty. Finding a quiet corner in the library and perusing *The Happy Hooker, Everything You Always Wanted to Know about Sex but Were Afraid to Ask*, and *The Sensuous Man* readied me for the onset of manhood that I was sure was just around the corner. It wasn't, but that's another story.

Then I discovered used-book stores—the best places to get discounted second-hand comics. (Those were the days when a giant *Superman* went for a quarter and vendors didn't know how valuable the vintage titles were.) Soon I was scanning the shelves for hidden treasures: a dog-eared copy of David Niven's exceptional memoir *The Moon's a Balloon*; Agatha Christie's last Poirot book, *Curtain*, missing its cover, but thankfully none of its pages; Stephen King's *'Salem's Lot*, filled with what I hope were coffee stains. (By the way, Steve, how can you write a thousand-page book every year? Come on. It's insane!) I can still smell that strange book smell that made me feel I had been transported back in time. There is no aroma that takes me back to a time of my life more vividly than the scent of a musty tome. Yeah, you read that right. Musty tome. Not only my rap name, but also an example of the only kind of writing I thought I was capable of before *Not Quite the Classics.*

Write a book? Me? (Question mark.)

It all started with my manager, Jeff Andrews, saying, "Col, why don't you write a book?" Jeff is constantly trying to get me to work. In the twenty years that he has represented me, he's never steered me wrong (except for that time he got me involved in a three-day New York dance recital where I had to play one of Cinderella's stepsisters in drag). It's one of the reasons I love him. Another reason is that he's the only person in the world I can say no to. So naturally when he brought up this idea, I said no. What would I write about? My life? I have been very fortunate and have had a wonderful life, but to be honest, it's really not that interesting. It would go something like this:

I was born. Grew up in the normal way. Got married to a beautiful woman, had a wonderful kid. Got a British TV show called *Whose Line is it Anyway?*, which became successful and moved to the U.S. All the cast members were good friends, so no Hollywood gossip there. It led to other work. The marriage is still happy, the boy is now a lovely young man, and ... here we are.

See? At most I could stretch it into a pamphlet. Undeterred, Jeff got me a literary agent, who secured a book deal.

I had to write a book. Damn. (Expletive.)

I knew for sure that this "book" would not be a novel. I wanted to incorporate my improv skills into this terrifying adventure, and as a practitioner of short scenes, short stories seemed the way to go. Then I was hit with a stroke of, if not genius, at the very least, high-functioning smarty-pantedness.

There is an improv game called First Line, Last Line, in which the beginning and the ending are supplied by the audience and the improvisers make up the rest. I could do *that* in a book. Take the first and last line of famous novels, make up the middle, and voila! So I found twelve classics with first and last lines that inspired me. That was tougher than it sounds. Many great novels have a terrific first line, but the last line can be a killer. Take, for example, Jane Austen's *Sense and Sensibility.*

First line: "The family of Dashwood had been long settled in Sussex."

Nice. Vague enough to go anywhere, but still has characters and a location.

Last line: "Between Barton and Delaford there was that constant communication which strong family affection would naturally dictate; and among the merits and the happiness of Elinor and Marianne, let it not be ranked as the least considerable, that though sisters, and living almost within sight of each other, they could live without disagreement between themselves, or producing coolness between their husbands."

That's pretty specific. It's also lengthy and dull.

So I went back to my first favourite: Dr. Seuss's *The Cat in the Hat.* My zombie version flowed out of me like one of those rare, perfectly improvised scenes. Other stories lurched and buckled. No flow. They were the dreaded *work.* Some surprised me, like the Sherlock Holmes tale, which needed the least amount of editing and was the most fun to write. Through it all, I learned something: I despised writing. Not the conjuring of the story, but the actual typing. My fingers could never keep up with my mind. (I believe this is what one would call a First World problem.) Still, I got through it, and with the end of every story came a feeling of accomplishment.

I couldn't have done it alone. Thanks to my wife, Debra McGrath, whose support and undying love definitely coloured some of the women found in this book. Thanks to my daughter, Kinley, without question my best work, who thinks I'm funny even when I'm not. To Jeff Andrews, for pushing me into this. To Carly Watters, my ever-supportive literary agent, whose notes and advice on my first three test stories were invaluable. To Adrienne Kerr, my editor, whose enthusiasm and gentle critique took me further than I thought I could go. To every author, published and unpublished, just for doing the work. Kudos!

And finally, to the writers whose lines I appropriated, thanks. I may not have read all your books, but I have seen all the movies.

So there you go. All the groaning and moaning, all the rewriting and editing, all the deadlines, missed and otherwise, are done.

I wrote a book! (Exclamation point.)

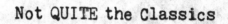

Not QUITE the Classics

A Study in Ha Ha

INSPIRED BY ARTHUR CONAN DOYLE'S
A STUDY IN SCARLET

Mr. Sherlock Holmes, who was usually very late in the mornings, save upon those not infrequent occasions when he was up all night, was seated at the breakfast table. His back was to me, but I could ascertain from his posture and almost preternatural stillness that he was working through some problem with that incredibly nimble mind of his. Mindful of how interruptions during this process would annoy the great consulting detective, I strove to show no sign of occupying the room.

"Watson, do sit down!" Holmes barked, in a tone equal parts irritation and patronizing dismissiveness. "You are one of the few people I know who can actually be more disruptive being stealthy. You're louder than a bagpiper at a Scottish wedding."

"I do apologize, Holmes, for disturbing you. But to be fair, I too am a tenant here and should be allowed space to breathe. Would you not agree?"

"It was not your breathing that alerted me to your presence," Holmes said dryly.

"What was it, then? Please do tell, so that I can endeavour to eradicate this predilection from my repertoire."

"Your sarcasm is duly noted. Those Oxfords you're

wearing emitted a C-sharp identical to a note that was misplayed during a performance by the Lower Slaughter String Quartet at a charity ball I was unfortunate enough to attend a fortnight ago."

I stood still for a moment processing the information. "Oh, you mean my shoes squeaked! Dear Lord in heaven, Holmes! It is a fortunate thing that our life expectancy is not shortened with each word we use, otherwise you would not have made it out of the nursery."

Holmes, quite surprisingly, smiled. "That was amusing, Watson."

"Oh. Ah ... thank you."

"Yes, quite amusing. The premise that life expectancy is inversely proportionate to loquaciousness, paired with the obviously silly supposition that I was a verbose toddler— yes. Quite amusing ..." Holmes trailed off, making some notes.

"Is there tea?" I inquired.

"Yes," Holmes muttered. "Here." He gestured to a side table.

I poured myself a cup and sat across from him. "Since I have interrupted you anyway, I suppose no harm could come of my asking you what is it that concerns you so. A new case, perhaps? Is Moriarty up to his old tricks? Or could it be some family crisis with Mycroft?"

"Watson," Holmes said, impatiently tapping his pipe in the ashtray, "would you like me to answer or do you wish to make endless suppositions based on not one fact in your possession?"

My sheepish silence was answer enough.

"Fine, then, let me illuminate you." With that, he

bounded out of his chair and, grabbing me by the arm, led me to the lamp on the far wall. Then he leaned back, crossed his arms, and laughed.

"Holmes, have you taken leave of your senses? What are you doing?"

"Why, Watson, I am *illuminating* you!"

I sneered. "Oh, I see. A pun, is it? I suppose you think that hilarious?"

"No. Though I was hoping for a more favourable reaction from you. What with the pun being the basest of all humour, I was sure that you would be affected in a highly positive way."

"Now look here, Holmes …" Before I could continue my protestation, he rushed back to his breakfast table and proceeded to scribble feverishly on some foolscap. I must confess that his behaviour was becoming increasingly irritating. I thought I had become quite inured to the eccentricities of my friend, but these ramblings, followed by bursts of physical exertion, were beyond the pale. "Holmes! I must insist that you inform me as to what the blazes is going on!"

Holmes looked up at me and, for the briefest of moments, smiled. He jumped from the chair and made his way to the fireplace, then whipped around to face me. Quite often, Holmes became very dramatic in the lead-up to one of his pronouncements. In this instance, he reminded me of Sarah Bernhardt about to launch into the "To be or not to be" soliloquy.

Holmes seemed to make a mental note of that, then spoke. "Watson, as you know, I get bored quite easily. Since there has been a paucity of truly challenging cases lately,

I have been dabbling in various experiments to keep my mind limber."

My eyes involuntarily darted to the spot where I had hidden his needles.

"I am not speaking of the *remedies* I employ to keep my spirits up."

I glanced at the liquor cabinet.

"Nor have I overindulged in any other vice, Watson. I think you shall be surprised when I tell you what has ignited my interest."

My eyes strayed to the spot where I had secreted some reading material that, though in my possession purely for scientific reasons, may be considered inappropriate even for gentlemen of the medical sciences.

"Watson, are you hiding anything else in our rooms? Your eyes are bulging and darting about like that of a stroke victim. It is very off-putting."

"Holmes, what is it? What is this new fascination?"

"Humour!"

"Humour?"

"Humour!"

"I'm afraid you've lost me."

"Last night, after supper, I became quite restless." His eyes fixed upon me with his customary intensity. "I tell you, Watson, you will never grasp what torture it is when I have nothing to occupy my mind. I cannot rest. I must always have something percolating. As I'm sure you are aware, I am often trying to perfect my ability to blend in at any event, in any location."

"Ah yes, your penchant for disguises."

"Correct. I had perfected a camouflage that would allow

me to go anywhere in the city and fit right in. I made my way to—"

"What was the disguise?" I asked.

"It makes no difference to what I'm about to tell you. I made my way to the Lambkin and Puffin, a boisterous pub in—"

"I'm sure it wasn't a beggar."

"What?"

"Your disguise. Not a beggar. You said it could get you anywhere. Being done up like a beggar would make you stand out in most quarters. A postman! No ... not at night, surely."

"As I said before, the disguise matters not. May I get on with my story, Watson?"

"A dog? A dog could be most places. Were you camouflaged as a dog?"

"Think, man! How could I pass as a dog?"

"Well, you'd have to remove your pipe."

"Madeline!"

"Excuse me?"

"Madeline was my disguise. A lady! Watson, I was dressed as a lady whom I have named Madeline. In this guise I could be anything from a lowly streetwalker to the wife of a well-to-do banker. Depending on station or location, of course."

At the thought of Holmes dressed as a woman, I became slightly ill. "Depending more on the amount of light, I should think."

"I'll have you know the disguise was a resounding success! I had many an admiring glance tossed my way ... Are you all right, old boy? You look a trifle green."

"No, no, I'm fine. Please finish your story."

"To test my disguise, I walked around joining various groups of revellers in escalating stages of drunkenness—the revellers, not I—and was drawn to one group in particular whose members were enthralled, listening to a large, portly fellow telling stories." Holmes paused, and his eyes seemed to burrow right through me. "*Funny* stories. Watson, I don't know if the stories were true, but they seemed so. They illumined our social mores, our intimate relationships with others, and all with a comical twist that quite accentuated our human foibles. Even I chortled at least twice and outright guffawed three times." Holmes fell silent.

I felt that I should add to the conversation. "Oh." It wasn't much, but it seemed to urge Holmes on.

"Then the most amazing thing happened! Amazing and infuriating. I said something in reply to one of the monologues, and the crowd, as if they were a single organism, laughed. A loud laugh. Watson, I have never experienced such a feeling. Every nerve ending seemed on fire, and I was flushed with some emotion that I still can't put a name to. It was as if some euphoric drug had just entered my bloodstream. It was ..."

It was the first time I could recall Holmes ever being speechless. It was most disturbing.

"Holmes, you said it was amazing *and* infuriating. Why infuriating?"

Holmes looked at me with almost haunted eyes. "I can't remember what I said. Not one part of it." He paused. "But this experience has spurred me on to a new endeavour. One that might actually bring me happiness. I call it ... stand-up comedy!"

"Stand-up comedy?"

"Yes. On the first Saturday of every month, the Lambkin and Puffin stages a talent show made up of the locals performing whatever party tricks they can devise. I will write ten to twenty minutes of highly humorous material and I will perform three weeks hence. I will write comedy and I will stand up as I interpret it. Stand-up comedy!"

A look of skepticism must have travelled my countenance, for Holmes fixed his gaze upon me.

"Yes, Watson? You have something to say?"

"Well, Holmes, I think that— What I mean to say is that— And this is coming from a place of friendship and nothing else. I certainly don't want to—"

"Spit it out, man!"

"You're not funny."

Holmes looked as though he had found a centipede in his cock-a-leekie. "Not. Funny?"

"Well, not in a humorous way, certainly. Your sarcasm can be amusing sometimes, if one is not the target of its venomous bite. But I certainly don't think of you as one of the great wits in my social sphere."

"You laughed at something I said only a few days ago at the grocers," Holmes said indignantly.

"Um. No. No, it was not what you said. It was when you banged your knee against the coconuts. It made a funny sound."

"Coconuts?"

"Yes, coconuts."

Holmes inspected his shoes for a few moments. "I must confess, Watson, you have hurt me in a manner I did not think possible."

"I do apologize ..."

"No. No need. It just spurs me on to prove you wrong. I believe I am up to the challenge." He ran to the calendar on the wall and circled a date. "On this day, a mere three weeks from now, I shall prove to you that I am, in fact, quite humorous. I shall expect you to be in the audience when I take to the stage."

"Certainly, Holmes, certainly."

"Then as the cannibal toymaker said to his friend, 'The game's a foot!'" Holmes stood there awaiting a reaction.

I could not give him the one he desired. "Perhaps you should stay away from puns." I smiled weakly.

Holmes glared and then made his way to his study, leaving me with a burgeoning sense of foreboding.

In the following days, Holmes kept to his study, writing furiously, collecting or discarding premises, joke structures, and other mysterious fancies. After one three-hour period hunkered down in his room, he bounded out with such vigour that I expected him to shout "Eureka!" and explain Archimedes' principle to me.

"It's mathematical, Watson! All *mathematical*!"

"I'm sure I would agree, Holmes, if in fact I knew what you were talking about."

"Comedy! It follows the same mathematical principles as music. It's all about rhythm and emphasis. Dah dah dah dah dah ... dah dah *dah* dah." He laughed.

"It might be funnier with actual words."

Before Holmes could dispatch a withering riposte, Mrs. Hudson appeared at the door.

"Mr. Holmes, a package has just come for—"

Before the poor woman could finish, Holmes had leapt towards her, grabbed the package, and begun ripping it open.

"Well, I never," she gasped.

"Now, Mrs. Hudson, I'm almost positive that that isn't true," Holmes retorted.

I'm not sure why, but I burst into laughter and was at once mortified. "Please excuse us, Mrs. Hudson, but we are in the middle of a case that is quite—"

"I don't want to know about it," she said. "I should have rented to accountants. They know how to treat a landlady, I'm sure." She left in a huff.

"Watson, it's come!" Holmes held aloft a leather-bound book, quite thick and possessing that intoxicatingly musty odour exuded by only the most ancient of tomes.

"What is it, Holmes?"

"This, my dear Watson, is the oldest joke book in existence. *Philogelos: The Laugh Addict.* Attributed to a pair of Greeks named Hierocles and Philagrius."

"Surely you can't be thinking of using these jokes! They were written centuries ago! How could any of this be relatable today? This certainly will not help your erected comedy."

"Stand-up comedy, Watson, stand-up. And you may be surprised to know that many of these jokes are still relatable to modern times. For example ..." He quickly leafed through the book.

"Ha! No, no ... That would only work if one knew that the ancients believed lettuce to be an aphrodisiac." He raised an eyebrow at me. "You didn't happen to know that, did you?"

"No, Holmes, I didn't. Is there any reason I should?"

"No, no, of course not. Oh, here we go. 'A misogynist is attending to the burial of his wife, who has just died, when someone asks: "Who is it who rests in peace here?" He answers: "Me, of course, now that I'm rid of her!"'"

I allowed myself a chuckle. "Yes, I see, Holmes. I suppose drolleries about matrimonial life remain relevant regardless of the age."

Holmes continued to leaf through the book "Not only matrimony but family relations, stupidity ..." He stopped at a page. "Even flatulence. Things still relevant today."

A notion struck me. "I have to say, though—harkening back to your mathematical theory of joke telling—that particular quip you just relayed seemed to have too many beats. It seems to have thrown off the rhythm."

"Well done, Watson! We'll make a thinking man of you yet."

"Now, there's no reason to—"

"I'm joking. You are right, there were too many syllables. Of course, I was translating from the original Greek, so I should be allowed some latitude. Watson, with my theories and with the aid of this learned tome, I may be on the brink of being funny."

"Dear God, Holmes, if this discovery falls into the wrong hands, civilization as we know it could end."

Holmes punctured the awkward silence. "Ah yes. Exaggerism: an exaggerated witticism that overstates the features, defects, or the strangeness of someone or something. Well played, Doctor, well played." And with that, he sprinted to his study.

I did not see him until two o'clock the next afternoon. He leapt out of his room. (During the period leading up to his performance, Holmes never just walked out of his study. He bounded, leapt, bobbed, hurtled, sprung, pounced, and one time, he gambolled.)

"Tell me, Doctor. Which is funnier: a goat or a duck?"

"I beg your pardon?"

"It's a simple query. Goat or duck?"

"Well ... duck."

At that, Holmes dropped down as if dodging a projectile. A few seconds later, he popped up. "Did you see what I did there? I mistook your meaning of duck and turned it into a humorous situation."

"Holmes, have you had any sleep?"

"No time. Awake or asleep, the duck misunderstanding is highly amusing. And you are right, duck is funnier. Do you know why?" Holmes raised an eyebrow.

"Because its alternative meaning allows you to do physical comedy."

"No, because it has a *k* in it."

"The letter *k* is funny, is it?"

"Not in and of itself. It's the k sound that prompts amusement. When a mouth forms the k in any word, it widens into a grin, subconsciously making those observing this smile along. Many words that are endowed with the k factor are among the most amusing in the English language. Think of it: knickers, scuttlebutt, spelunking."

"I have to admit, I always have to conceal a smirk when introduced to a Kenneth."

I studied Holmes's tired face. "Would you like me to make you something to eat? I can't remember the last time I saw you indulge in foodstuffs."

"Thank you, Watson, that is very considerate."

"What would you like?"

"It's obvious." He smiled. "Kippers, of course!"

The next day, as I was going over some particularly intriguing anatomical texts, Holmes barrelled out of his room.

"Watson! Knock, knock."

"Ah! Ha ha … yes, very funny, Holmes."

"What is?"

"Your two k sounds. Yes, quite amusing."

"No, no, this is a different thing altogether. Knock, knock."

I stared at him.

"Knock, knock," Holmes repeated.

"Why do you keep saying 'Knock, knock'?"

"It's something I have just invented. Well, to be truthful, I borrowed it from Shakespeare. The Porter … from *Macbeth*. Are you familiar with it?"

"Yes, Holmes, I am. I'm not illiterate, you know. I have read plays and books. You may have seen me with a newspaper at times."

"All right, all right. No need to get your dander up. The Porter in the Scottish play pretends to be the porter to the gates of hell welcoming sinners of different professions. All follow the pattern of 'Knock, knock,' to which comes the reply 'Who's there?' Then comes the joke. In the play it was a monologue, but I have devised it so that the audience can become part of the fun."

"How will they know to say 'Who's there?'"

Holmes seemed nonplussed. "What?"

"How," I said, unconsciously slowing down as if talking to a Frenchman or a somewhat addled cocker spaniel, "will the audience know to say 'Who's there?'"

"I shall tell them. That does not matter at the moment. I am trying to work the concept to see if the format is successful."

"All right. Who's there?"

"Wait for the set-up, will you? Knock, knock."

"Yes?"

"Not 'yes.' 'Who's there?' Let's start again, shall we?" Holmes sighed loudly. "Knock, knock."

"Who's there?" I said.

"'Tis I, Sherlock Holmes. Don't you recognize me?"

I stood stock-still, not knowing how to respond. Holmes, too, seemed a little uncertain.

"Hmm," he said. "There's something missing ... but what? What? Of course! There's no familiarity with the concept, so there can be no deconstruction at this particular ... hmm." He trailed off, lost in thought. "Watson, after I say who is at the door, repeat the name I give you, adding the word 'who.'"

"All right, Holmes."

"Knock, knock."

"Who's there?"

"Sherlock."

"Sherlock who?"

Affecting a perfect Irish accent, Holmes replied, "Sure, lock the door so I can't get in."

I laughed. Heaven help me, I laughed. I have never seen Holmes's face so lit up as when he heard that laugh. It worried me.

And so it was for the days leading up to Holmes's debut as a standing up comedian. Just as I was growing accustomed to his prolonged absences, he would launch himself from his study talking about the science of eliciting laughter. If you have never had to sit through such a lecture, I can tell you it is the driest, most mind-numbing subject ever. The worst part of the whole process was that Holmes seemed physically unable to let any word, phrase, or idea pass by without turning it into a joke. It was most annoying. The closer the day of his performance drew, the more high-strung he became. The foreboding I felt would not leave me.

The fateful day arrived. Holmes was not about when I made my way to breakfast. A cursory search of the flat did not turn him up. There was, however, a note.

> Watson
>
> I shall see you tonight at the show. Please wish good thoughts for me.
>
> I fear that all may not go according to plan.

The sick feeling in my stomach grew acute.

That evening I made my way to the Lambkin and Puffin.

It was not located in the most savoury of neighbourhoods, yet it was pleasantly appointed and the ale was better than many of the higher-class public houses I frequented. I looked around for Holmes, but he was nowhere to be seen. For a brief moment I entertained the thought that perhaps he had thought better of this venture. Then again, I thought, Sherlock Holmes had faced dangers that would make the stoutest of men blanch. Surely reciting comic material in a pub before a drunken crowd would not unnerve him?

The master of ceremonies, a coarse, affable type, introduced the first act: an immense matron whose repertoire of light opera ditties enthralled the audience— for two or three songs. After the fifth, she was booed handily and left the stage in tears. She was followed by a dog act, an acrobat, and a man who performed various bird whistles from his posterior. At last, it was time for Holmes. He received hearty applause, for he had acquired some fame in these parts, having solved a missing persons case involving a popular local merchant. My heart sank as I saw him walk on stage. He had the telltale signs of having indulged in his favourite vice. I swore silently to myself. Cocaine and comedy could not be a good mix.

Holmes spoke: "Thank you for the kind welcome. I must admit I didn't think I would get here in time. You see, my dog, a lovely Rottweiler, has a bit of a physical impediment. As a caring master, I took him to the veterinarian. 'My dog's cross-eyed. Is there anything you can do for him?' 'Well,' says the vet, 'let's have a look at him.' He picks the dog up and examines his eyes, then checks his teeth. Finally, he says, 'I'm going to have to put him down.' I was aghast. 'What? You have to put my dog down because he's cross-eyed?' 'No,' said the veterinarian, 'I have to put him down because he's heavy.'"

The audience laughed robustly. Then Holmes did something I have never seen him do. He giggled. It was quite inappropriate and not a little unmanly. It seemed to take the audience aback. Holmes appeared not to notice as he launched into his second story.

"My landlady, Mrs. Hudson, also had a bit of a health crisis. She told her doctor, 'I've got a bad back.' The doctor said, 'It's old age.' She said, 'I want a second opinion.' So the doctor said, 'Certainly. You're ugly too.'" Holmes giggled once more.

I have to say I was not in the least amused. Mrs. Hudson, while perhaps not the greatest beauty in London, is nevertheless not ugly. I was quite relieved that she had decided not to see Holmes in his inaugural performance. The next joke did little to appease my growing uneasiness.

"As an expert in various subjects, I am often asked to give lectures to committees and the like. Once I was asked by the Women's Institute to give a talk about sex. I didn't mind agreeing to give the talk, but I was a bit worried that my friend and biographer Dr. Watson wouldn't like me doing it. He is very prudish about subjects dealing with intimacy."

What an outrageous lie! But since I had not a voice in these proceedings, I was forced to sit and bear this gross injustice.

"So as to spare his feelings, I told the dear doctor that I was engaged to talk to the Women's Institute on the subject of sailing. The day after my lecture, Watson bumped into the chairwoman of the Women's Institute. 'I thought the talk Mr. Holmes gave last night was quite excellent!' said the chairwoman. 'He certainly seemed an expert on the subject!' 'Did he?' asked the doctor. 'I'm quite surprised! He hardly knows anything about it. He's only done it twice. The first time he was sick and the second time his hat blew off!'"

The audience laughed at first, and then the greater implications of the story seemed to dawn on them: that I knew all about Holmes's intimacies either through his confidence or through personal knowledge. Holmes had called into question the nature of our friendship, making it the butt of his joke. He seemed to grasp this at about the same time the audience did. Again he giggled, this time with a higher pitch than before. The more he giggled, the less the audience laughed. But Holmes noticed this too late. Beads of perspiration congregated into rivulets of sweat that rolled down his face.

"Uh. I was … no … A man was …" Holmes stopped, his eyes filled with a panic that I never would have thought possible. He had the stunned expression of a Cockney in Greece. He started to pace.

The audience murmured restlessly. One wag at the back shouted, "Come on, 'Olmes. Get on wi' it!"

Holmes gamely kept on with his performance. But in his agitation he seemed to lose his bearings. He was in the midst of remembering what he was to say when he overstepped the stage. In mid-fall he exclaimed, "Oh sweet dear Lord!" then plummeted to the ground.

I am ashamed to say that I burst out laughing, along with the rest of the patrons. Holmes's proper demeanour, coupled with the pratfall, was one of the funniest things I had ever seen. I rushed to help my friend, wiping the tears from my eyes. He looked at me with humiliation etched on his brow and through clenched teeth, growled, "Get me out of here, Watson! Now!"

We left to gales of uncontrolled laughter.

After his disastrous performance, Holmes would not leave his study. My entreaties went unheard; the food left at his door went untouched. Three days after his public humiliation, I lost my temper.

Standing at the door to his hideaway, I spoke: "Holmes! This behaviour is childish and petulant. I regret that your attempt at stand-up comedy was not as you planned, but for heaven's sake, man, that is what life is. Not everything can be as you wish it. Can we not look at the positive? You are to be commended for your courage in attempting something that is as foreign to you as fighting a war is to the French. There is no shame in failing in this endeavour, not with all that you have, the many skills that leave men envious of your talent. Buck up, me bucko. Just buck up!"

There was silence from beyond the door, then Holmes's familiar voice rang out. "Buck up, me bucko?" He laughed. A good, long laugh. "I had come to the same conclusion as you, my dear friend," he called out. "It is foolish to think that I should be a jack of all trades. Best to concentrate on what I do best and leave comedy to those who are expert in it. I want to thank you for the support that you have given me throughout this fool's errand. As a reward, would you be my guest at tonight's performance of the Russian Ballet's highly praised production of *Swan Lake*? The only condition is that we never speak of this again and that you not publish this particular adventure until I'm dead."

"You have my word, Holmes," I called through the door.

"Excellent."

The door opened and Holmes stepped out. Or should I say, Madeline stepped out. She was dressed to the nines and quite attractive (in a most uncanny manner, I should clarify). It was a remarkable disguise, capable of fooling the most discerning gentlemen.

"Might I trouble you then to be ready in half an hour, and we can stop at Marcini's for a little dinner on the way?"

Moby: Toupée or Not Toupée

INSPIRED BY HERMAN MELVILLE'S
MOBY-DICK

"Call me, Ishmael."

It took Ishmael a few seconds to recognize who had left the truncated message on his cell phone. His agent, Jeff, he realized, with a mixture of relief and indigestion. (He'd hoovered a cup of probiotic yogourt outside the Pilates studio. He wasn't sure if it was the Activia or the roll-ups and single-leg circles that had brought on the nausea.) It had been almost a month since Ishmael had been out on an audition. It had been a slow year, a very slow year. A corpse on *CSI*, a one-line waiter part on *Bones*, and a crying mourner on *House* were all the credits he had to show for twelve months of auditions, play readings, and showcase variety gigs. It was *ridiculous*. He looked into the rear-view mirror and stretched his lips. "It *was* ridiculous. *It* was ridiculous." He smoothed an unruly, Andy Rooney–esque eyebrow and signalled a left-hand turn on Augusta. There were times Ishmael had trouble accepting the fact that his chosen profession was so unfair. He was a very good actor, had gotten great reviews in recent local productions, was a master of pretending at getting along with people, and yet he still had to hustle for decent parts. Part of him, at least a full three-quarters, had trouble believing he wasn't ranked alongside De Niro, Pacino, and Streep by now. The journey to superstardom starts with one small step, he reminded himself. At least he was getting another audition.

He autodialed Jeff. After he repeated his name to the receptionist, she put him through.

"Hey, Ish. Last-minute audition for today, two o'clock at Caster's. Commercial, national. Pretty straightforward. Spokesperson, warm, friendly, blah blah blah. For Chicken in a Can."

"Oh, a commercial?"

"Well, beggars can't be choosy." Jeff had a way with clichés.

"All right. What's the spot about?"

"A young man and his father open up emotionally over a hearty helping of Chicken in a Can. The usual. You're reading for the father."

It took a few seconds for Ishmael to register what Jeff meant. "Father? How old is the son?"

"Mid-twenties."

"Mid-twenties? But I'm only thirty-four. Is my character a hillbilly? I can't have a son that old."

"Logically, yeah. But, you know ... you do look older."

"I look perfectly good. I look younger than thirty-four in my opinion ... and others ... have that opinion ..."

"Ish, face it. You're just one of those guys who look older when they lose their ... When they become ... You know ..."

"Bald?" Ishmael exclaimed, shrilly. "What, I lose my hair and I'm Wilford Brimley all of a sudden? So what's left for me? Quaker Oats ads and Viagra infomercials?"

"Hey, life's unfair. Suck it up. You want this audition?"

"Yes," he said, a tad petulantly.

"Okay, then. I'll email you the script and the details. Good luck."

Jeff hung up on him.

When he got home, Ishmael was still incensed. This is how I'm being defined as an actor, he thought incredulously, stepping into the shower. The bald guy who looks older than his years. Maybe I should update my résumé. Ishmael Moby—Caucasian, brown eyes, bald. Under his special skills (which included juggling, horseback riding, and squash—three things he had never done in his life), he could add: Can play twice my chronological age.

As he towelled off, Ishmael wiped the steam from the bathroom mirror and took a long, hard look at his reflection. I do look older. If I could only afford a better exfoliant, he thought. That's the only reason I look a little weathered. But mostly, he had to admit, the aging was due to the premature grey. More salt than pepper now. The horseshoe haircut didn't help. He was a good-looking man with a strong chin, great cheekbones, and flawless skin. Unfortunately, the skin went a little higher on his head than he would have liked. Ishmael thought that he had come to terms with his hair loss, but obviously he had been fooling himself. But he wasn't the one who needed to come to terms with it. Casting directors were. It was unfair that society couldn't look past a lack of hair, even more unfair that the entertainment industry couldn't. Ishmael equated his struggle with that of Hattie McDaniel, the first

African American to win an Oscar. Except for the major differences, their stories were identical.

Ishmael's audition was only a fifteen-minute walk away, but he started to make his way there an hour before his scheduled time. He was notoriously early for everything—auditions, parties, medical appointments. Partly because he thought it showed enthusiasm and a willingness to get down to it, partly because he usually had the time.

As he turned onto Macauley, a tree-lined boulevard full of shops and cafés, he noticed a store that hadn't been there before. Under a green-and-blue striped awning, the sign on the window read "Hair by Rachel" in a lovely serif font. Ishmael looked through the leaded panes at artfully displayed mannequin heads, bedecked with toupées, wigs, and extensions. They were unlike anything Ishmael had ever seen before. They looked incredibly real—no, *better* than real. They looked alive. Silky, glossy hair, of every colour and style. One took Ishmael's interest right away. It matched his natural Manila Ice Chocolate brown shade perfectly and looked so luxurious he was overcome with a desire to walk barefoot through it. Ishmael stood there for a full thirty minutes transfixed by its beauty. The sign on the door said "Closed," or else he might have gone in. He finally managed to tear himself away and reluctantly crossed the street to his audition.

Ishmael's heart sank when he walked into Caster's. It looked like Yul Brynner Tribute Day. About thirty men, in various stages of hair loss, paced around, practising varied interpretations of the line "It's Chicken in a Can!" On the other side of the room, another group waited for a different audition. Not a chrome-dome in the bunch.

In fact, if you put a line straight down the middle of the room, it looked like a before-and-after shot for Rogaine. The only thing both groups had in common was the reek of desperation.

"Hey, Moby!"

Ishmael cringed. Jackie Fleming! Fleming was a constant pain in Ishmael's ass. He was always competing for the same parts, though he was a completely different physical type. Fleming was a big man, close to three hundred pounds, if not more. Three of those pounds may have been actual muscle; the rest was two hundred and ninety-seven pounds of comfortable living. His head was the size of a baby Rottweiler and was stuck onto a body that looked similar to the Pillsbury Doughboy's, if Poppin' Fresh had totally let himself go. Ishmael didn't know how the two of them actually ended up competing for the same parts, but it seemed to happen all the time. Fleming usually came out on top and he was never a gracious winner. Ishmael despised him.

"Hey, Fleming. What are you auditioning for?"

"Movie of the Week. Third billed. Could be really good."

"Great," Ishmael said, relieved. He forced his lips into what he hoped was a supportive smile.

"You part of the Shiny Brigade?"

Ishmael's blood began to boil. His hands clenched and unclenched as he tried to control his temper. "Yes. I am part of that group." He started to turn away.

"No kidding. Should have worn my sunglasses. The glare ... my God, the glare."

Ishmael whipped around and thrust his head a few inches from Fleming's. "Really, Fatso?"

Someone gasped. One of the hirsute group. Ishmael spun on them.

"Really? That was worth a gasp, was it? He does five minutes of bald jokes and that's okay? But I make one fat joke and I'm the insensitive one?"

"It's genetic," Fleming mumbled.

"Genetic if your parents hated salads!" Ishmael pointed to his head. "What do you think this is? You think I shave my head every day into this lovely horseshoe pattern because I'm a Secretariat fan? Why is it fine to make fun of us? Why aren't bald people protected by the politically correct!"

Shouts of "Tell it, brother!" and "Shame the hairies!" rang out from the other side of the room. All of a sudden, Ishmael didn't care about the audition; he just wanted to get out of there before he started beating on Fleming with one of the folding chairs in the corner. He ran from the room.

Out on the sidewalk, Ishmael braced his hands on his knees and took long breaths trying to calm himself down. He started for home, but then saw that the sign on Rachel's door had been flipped around to "Open." He crossed the street and stood beneath the awning to gaze in the window. The exquisite hairpiece called to him, like a siren seducing an ancient mariner, "Try me, try me, try me."

What the hell, Ishmael thought, I just screamed at a fat man in a room full of people. Walking into a hair store is going to embarrass me? He pushed the door open, and the bell over the door tinkled merrily. There was no one around. Good, he thought. Last thing I need is a pushy salesperson.

The toupée was even more breathtaking up close. The light from the window caught the strands and made it shimmer. He wanted it. He touched it, and his hand shook with desire.

"Nice, isn't it?"

Ishmael spun around. Behind the counter stood a woman who could have been anywhere between forty and seventy. Her eyes were black as coal and shifted rapidly from side to side. She had the most untrustworthy face he had ever seen, but her hair was spellbinding. Definitely her best feature, though to be truthful, it didn't have much competition. It was jet black, full, and silky, and it moved with an almost lyrical beauty with every head tilt. She was like a better-coiffed Medusa.

"Beautiful," she said, pointing to the toupée. "That one's my baby."

"Your baby?"

"All of them are my babies. I gave birth to them. Metaphorically speaking." Her eyes ceased their roving and bored into his. "It took months to make them, strand by strand."

"You must be Rachel."

"Yes, I must." She grinned lopsidedly, flashing dull teeth. "Are you interested in adoption?"

"Adoption?"

"Yes. You do not buy my babies, you must adopt them. They give so much more when they know they are loved. It's just simple paperwork. A quick signature and presto."

Hmm, Ishmael thought, loony-tune. He smiled slowly so as not to alarm her.

"Well, I am interested in … uh … adopting. How much does this one cost?"

Rachel stroked the side of her face. "Ten thousand."

Ishmael's heart stopped. "Ten thousand dollars?"

"My babies are of the highest quality. This little beauty will be the only hairpiece you will need for the rest of your life. It will grow with you, go grey with you."

"How is that possible?"

"It's possible." Rachel looked away and her eyes resumed their flickering.

"Ten thousand dollars," Ishmael repeated. "I can't. That's … a little beyond my budget."

"Oh, that's too bad." Rachel picked up a newspaper and trained her eyes on the text. Ishmael wondered how she could read. He turned and headed to the exit and his eyes took in the toupée one last time. His heart beat like a snare drum as he pulled open the door. Rachel laughed softly behind him.

For the rest of the day Ishmael was consumed by thoughts of the toupée. He thought about it as he ran off some new résumé shots. He worried about it all through his shift at the Steer and Stein. He obsessed about it during his "Audition with Balls" workshop. I've got to have it, Ishmael thought, but ten thousand dollars! He'd have to forget about it. He had no access to that kind of money.

But he couldn't forget about it. He dreamt about it that night. Dreams of how it could transform his life.

The next day Ishmael decided to go back to Rachel's and see if he could set up a payment plan. The worst that could happen was that she might say no. As he turned onto Macauley, he saw Rachel on the sidewalk in front of the store sweeping up broken glass.

"What happened?"

She turned to him with ping-pong hate-filled eyes.

"Robbery. Someone stole my babies."

Technically, that would be kidnapping, but Ishmael felt that Rachel wouldn't care for the distinction. He looked into the store through the smashed window. His toupée no longer occupied its prime spot. Most of the inventory was gone.

"Do you have any idea who did it?"

Rachel kept her eyes still long enough to look at him disdainfully. "A ring of bald thieves, I suppose. I saw many of *your kind* across the street there, yesterday. Perhaps the lure of luxuriant hair overcame them."

"Don't be ridiculous! They're actors. Actors don't steal."

Rachel smiled coldly, and made Ishmael shiver. "It makes no nevermind. I will get them back. All my babies will be returned. Every single one of them." She snorted and went back to sweeping glass.

Ishmael walked back the way he had come, confused and depressed. It wasn't so much the theft of beautiful toupées that saddened him, but the thought that someone else would be wearing his hair. The thought that someone else had taken his baby and would be sharing those special father/baby hair moments filled him with deep despair.

As he passed an alley, he heard a familiar voice.

"Try me."

He stopped and peered down the alley but saw no one. He was just about to move on when he noticed a box partly obscured by a recycling bin. He could make out the lettering on the side of the box: "achel." He ran to the box, squatted, and with trembling hands opened it. His toupée gleamed softly inside. Ishmael could swear it purred for a second. But how? And what of that voice that called out to him? Could it have been ...? Ishmael laughed. Yeah, that's it, he thought, the hair called out to me. It wants me. He laughed again, a little desperately, a little afraid. But full of hope. Holding the box tightly to his chest, he ran all the way home. It wasn't till he was inside the apartment and standing at his kitchen counter, breathless, that he thought perhaps he should have returned the hair to Rachel. He felt a little sick to his stomach.

He immediately came up with a hundred reasons why he shouldn't return the hair. The main one was that he didn't want to. The hair was his.

Ishmael took the box into his bedroom, where the lighting was best. When he looked in the mirror with his new do, he wanted the full impact. He gently removed the hair from the box and turned it this way and that. Doesn't look as impressive out of the store, he thought. He placed it on his head. It fit like a glove, like a head glove. But Ishmael was disappointed when he looked in the mirror. The Ishmael reflected back at him was just the same old Ishmael with a toupée on. Was he insane to hope that it might actually have transformed him? He sighed.

I'll give it back to Rachel, he thought. Maybe I'll get a reward. But just as he was about to put the toupée back in the box, he noticed a piece of parchment at the bottom. Pulling it out, he saw it was an adoption paper for the hairpiece. Ishmael remembered what Rachel had said:

"You do not buy my babies, you must adopt them. They give so much more when they know they are loved."

Ishmael looked over the papers. Seemed like your normal adoption contract, as if he would know the difference. He took a pen from his nightstand and signed on the dotted line. Why not? Couldn't hurt.

Ishmael put the toupée back on his head and right away felt a difference. It seemed to hug his skull and it felt warm and soothing up there. Looking in the mirror, he almost burst into tears. He was a handsome man with a full head of hair. A new Ishmael. No matter how closely he scrutinized his head, from every angle, he could not see where his hair ended and the rug began. It looked like his hair! His body surged with energy and confidence that he had not felt in years, and his eyes sparkled.

"Looking good, baby," he said aloud, snapping his fingers at his reflection. "Looking gooood." He was immediately embarrassed by his cheesiness but couldn't resist one more admiring glance.

The next three weeks of Ishmael's life were golden. He booked two commercials, three major guest spots on popular TV shows, and the lead in a movie to be shot in France in the summer. His love life perked up too. Women noticed him, and were charmed by his humour. He brought home one girl who remarked, after, "You make love like an ugly man. You know, you're *grateful*. It's so refreshing."

Thank God everybody was so shallow, thought Ishmael delightedly. Yes, things were going beautifully. Well, mostly beautifully.

He had to admit that a few odd things had happened recently. A couple of nights after he started wearing the rug, while Ishmael was preparing himself for bed, he placed the toupée on the Styrofoam head that was on the nightstand, admired it for a few minutes, and climbed beneath the covers. In a few minutes he was fast asleep.

The next morning he awoke to the sun streaming though his curtains. He stretched and made his way into the bathroom. As Ishmael passed the mirror, he did a double take. The toupée was on his head. He stopped and thought back to the night before. He was sure he had taken it off; in fact he was positive. Was he sleepwalking? It's second nature putting it on, he thought. I probably went to pee in the middle of the night and put it on then. He didn't quite manage to convince himself. He also didn't have a plausible explanation why the following day he found the toupée on the couch in front of the TV with a half-drunk can of beer beside it.

Ishmael didn't dwell on it, mainly because he was enjoying his life too much. When his commercials hit the airwaves, his career exploded. Jeff was calling every day with auditions and, best of all, straight offers. Things were looking up.

He started wearing the toupée all the time, not only for auditions and forays outside the apartment but 24/7. He immediately got new headshots, accentuating his luscious locks. He found that with his hair on, little perks came his way. Extra cinnamon in his Cinnamon Dolce Latte with soy milk. Complimentary starch in his dry-cleaned shirts. Memories of what it had been like to be bald fell away like his treacherous former hair. He was a new man.

Ishmael had an audition for a new series. Jeff said it was just a formality and that the part was his, but the producers just wanted to be sure. As he entered the casting room, he saw his old nemesis, Fleming, reading over the script. One of the most satisfying by-products of having hair was beating Fleming out on every audition.

"Hey, Jackie! How's things?"

Fleming looked up with barely disguised hate.

"Good."

"That's great, really great. Auditioning for the series, are you? Good luck with that."

"Hey, Ishmael, I've been wondering. Where'd you get the wig?"

Suddenly, as though someone whispered in his ear, Ishmael heard the words "Kill him!"

"Uh ... what?"

"The toup. I have a friend who could use one and I thought you could recommend the place you got yours. I thought maybe you got it at Rachel's, but then I remembered you showed up with it *after* it got robbed of all its merchandise. So it couldn't be from there ... could it?"

"Kill him," insisted the voice.

"No ... No, not Rachel's. It was a place I found on the internet. I'll get you the link."

"Yeah ... weird, though, right? Place gets robbed and the next day, you have a head of hair."

"KILL HIM!" yelled the voice.

Ishmael clenched his fists. It took every bit of effort he had not to put his hands around Fleming's throat and squeeze the life out of him. Just picturing it filled him with joy. Watching his eyes bulge out, Fleming's hands clutching at Ishmael's, trying to loosen his grip. Watching Fleming's fat life slip away. Ishmael shook off the fantasy, and then he realized he wasn't imagining it, he was doing it. He felt himself forcibly pulled off Fleming by a couple of actors. He watched helplessly as Fleming, red-faced, fell to the floor spluttering.

"What? What the fu ..."

Ishmael stared in horror at his hands, and turned and ran out of the room.

What was that?

What *the hell* was that?

When he got home, he pulled the toupée off his head. It was a struggle, as though the rug didn't want to go. Ishmael was scared, more terrified than he had ever been in his life. He was hearing voices—correction—*one voice*, telling him to kill Fleming, and he was almost certain that the voice belonged to the rug. It's evil, he realized, and thought of Rachel's flickering eyes. He almost giggled at the absurdity of it. He put the toupée back in the box and shoved it in his closet. He locked the door.

He went to his liquor cabinet and poured a glass of bourbon, downed it in one gulp. The phone rang and he jumped. He picked it up and in the steadiest voice he could muster he said, "Hello?"

"How's my lovely baby treating you?"

Ishmael could almost hear her eyes darting.

"Rachel?" he whispered.

"I've found all the others. Yours is the last."

"Mine? I'm sorry, I don't understand what you're talking about. Surely you're not accusing me of stealing a wig!"

"You *are* a good actor, aren't you? A nice mixture of indignation, hurt, and anger. Yes. I knew you were a good actor when I saw your commercial. You've changed a bit since I saw you last."

Ishmael winced. He hadn't even thought that Rachel might see his work.

"I don't have your hair. The one I have is ..." He trailed off. "So what did you see me in? The Robitussin bit? Or—"

"You can't fool a mother. Never fool a mother. See you soon."

Ishmael hung up and ran to the closet. He had to get rid of that rug before that crazy woman showed up. As he bent down to open the box, he faltered. What if I keep it? he thought. So what if it fills me with homicidal thoughts now and again? I mean, the work I've been getting! Ishmael caught himself and took a deep breath. No, I can't start killing people just so I can look good on camera. He opened the box.

It was empty. Ishmael's bowels clenched. Immediately he was covered in sweat. Not light perspiration. Heavy, heavy sweat.

From the top shelf of the closet, the toupée jumped onto Ishmael's head like a flying squirrel. Ishmael could feel the rug tighten its unholy grip on his scalp when he tried to rip it off. The harder he pulled, the harder it clung to his skull. With a strength born from desperation, Ishmael managed to tear it off his head and throw it to the floor. He screamed in horror when he saw little pieces of his scalp attached to it. He ran to the mirror and examined his head. Blood ran down his face from the small divots in his scalp.

"Son of a bitch! I have an on-camera audition tomorrow!"

He ran back to the bloody toupée and stomped on it as though it were a bug.

"Wear me! Wear me!" The words rang through his head in time with the stomping.

"Shut up! Shut up!" Ishmael stomped until the toupée was in tatters. Clumps of hair lay lifeless on the broadloom. Looking at it, Ishmael was overcome with remorse. It still looks good, he sobbed to himself. Maybe it can be trained to be non-homicidal. Maybe ... Ishmael shook himself from his crazed reverie. "Get out of my head!" he screamed. Out of the corner of his eye, he saw the stove, and a half-remembered made-for-TV horror movie came to mind. Something with Karen Black and a murderous doll. He ran to the stove and turned the oven on to broil. He ran back to the spot where he had unleashed his rage. The toupée was gone.

A little trail of loose hairs led under the sofa. Ishmael went to the couch and knelt down.

"Come on, baby. Come to Daddy."

He started feeling around underneath the couch. He patted the carpet, grasping for strands of Manila Ice Chocolate brown. Then he felt a sharp pain in his hand and he cried out. He yanked his hand back and gasped at a deep bite mark on his index finger.

It bit him! The little bastard bit him!

Ishmael ran to the kitchen and got his biggest carving knife. Kneeling carefully in front of the couch, he wildly stabbed the dark underneath. He waited. Nothing. Slowly, slowly he looked under the couch, but could see nothing. Then, Ishmael raised his head to the height of the sofa cushion and out of the corner of his eye, saw the toupée sitting, hairs crossed, in the armchair. Before he could react, the rug pounced.

"Not the face! Not the face!"

The toupée clung like a starfish, suffocating him. Struggling to breathe, Ishmael got out a muffled, "I'm your father!," but to no avail. He gulped for air that never came. He heard the door of his apartment opening, softly. His last thought was: I hope they don't give my part to Fleming.

Then he was still.

The person who had entered Ishmael's apartment walked over to his body, gently removed the toupée from his face, and put it in a fur-lined pouch. Her eyes flickered as she gazed about the room.

It was the devious-cruising Rachel, that in her retracing search after her missing children, only found another orphan.

Casey at the Bar

INSPIRED BY ERNEST THAYER'S
"CASEY AT THE BAT"

The Outlook wasn't brilliant for the Mudville nine that day:
The score stood four to two, with but one inning more to play ...
The side struck out, all hopes were dashed—so close and yet so
    far...
Then someone turned the TV off at Sam McCluskey's bar.

With Happy Hour just starting and the room devoid of cheer,
Disappointed patrons drowned their sorrows in their beer.
Mudville is a baseball town, through their team they live and die.
It doesn't matter much to me, for I'm a hockey guy.

Been a fan since '64, when there only were six teams.
Drank champagne from the Stanley Cup (though only in my
    dreams).
The league now numbers thirty, and not that I'm berating—
But two are now in Florida, a state not known for skating.

Having seen so many games in the fifty years that passed,
And versed in hockey trivia—can't be stumped by what I'm asked.
I know the players' faces, from Dick Duff to Bobby Orr.
So imagine my surprise, seeing Casey at the door.

He strode into McCluskey's, as the jukebox played Adele.
He hadn't really changed much, since he left the NHL.
The greatest goalie of his time—he could have been, hands
    down...
Instead all went astray, and they ran Casey out of town.

He was a goalie phenom rated highly by the scouts;
He was superstar material, of that there were no doubts.
Toronto celebrated. He was drafted by the Leafs!
"We'll win the Stanley Cup now!" was the popular belief.

Fans all hoped that this was true: it was time to dry their
    tears;
They hadn't tasted victory in over forty years.
Could this Casey spur the team? At that thought, the fans
    did foam...
Could this finally be the year that the Stanley Cup came
    home?

The promise started early with a ten-game winning streak.
The way the team was playing, not one person could
    critique.
The forwards, they were scoring. All believed the hype:
This team could not be beaten, not with Casey 'tween the
    pipes.

Nailed the Eastern Conference, due to Casey's acrobatics.
Playoff fever swept through town; it really was dramatic.
Casey took the league by storm, he was the King of Hockey.
And then, oh-oh, it all went south, for Casey became cocky.

He was growing quite conceited, which much concerned
    the Leafs.
Case in point: website photos of Casey in his briefs.
Without expressing sorrow as other people would;
He arrogantly smiled, and said, "Man, I'm looking good."

The team got through the first round, then the second and
    the third.
It almost felt too easy, these playoffs were absurd.
They made it to the finals, every hockey team's one wish.
Casey said, "We'll win in four! All comers we will squish."

This spurred the opposition, as the Leafs fans feared it
    would—
The Penguins won the first game. (Casey wasn't very good.)
The Leafs bounced back the next match, they won the third
    one too,
The Penguins ruled the next one, scoring five on you know
    who.

The fifth went to the Penguins, but the next was theirs to
    lose.
A seventh game was needed. Who would win? Too hard to
    choose.
Leafs fans, ever hopeful that the Cup would come their way,
Longed with such intensity that even atheists prayed.

The hockey game was started, back and forth the teams
    did skate.
Both played their very best, every player pulled his weight.
It came to pass the score was tied, one minute left to play.
Surely there'd be overtime. Oh no!—a breakaway!

An errant pass was picked up by a player from Pittsburgh,
He headed for the net, but Casey didn't seem perturbed.
He calmly touched the goalposts with his custom-made
    Sher-Wood,
Then gliding to his crease's edge, there mighty Casey
    stood.

The Penguins lad raced closer—the fans were on their feet.
Thousands screamed their lungs out, "Casey, don't get
    beat!"
Casey spun upon his skates, then bowing to the crowd,
Slipped and lost his balance, falling hard and big and loud.

The Penguin shot, he scored the goal, then jumped in
    celebration.
Boos rang out, they said it all: crushed hopes of a Leafs
    Nation.
"Casey, Casey, what a bum!" The crowd was all agreeing.
Don Cherry ranted from the booth: "He must be European!"

The newspapers were vicious; the fans called for his blood.
From hero down to scapegoat, Casey's name had become
    mud.
He was run right out of town, speeding in his fancy car.
That was the last I saw him till he walked into this bar.

Turning to the barkeep: "What's the story with that guy?"
I gestured then to Casey, who was giving girls the eye.
The barkeep looked and smiled, "Mr. Casey is his name.
He comes here every night, leaving with a different dame.

"The women they all love him, and the men, they all turn
    green.
For Casey, mighty Casey, is the best they've ever seen.
He might not be most handsome, and not the very
    smartest,
But that there Mr. Casey is a mighty pickup artist."

I watched as Casey sauntered by the tables where girls sat,
His eyes searched out the talent, like a horny alley cat.
He circled very slowly round the barroom, no mistake.
His movements showed to everyone: Casey's on the make.

So easy was his manner as he walked around the place,
He took his time just looking, knowing love was not a race.
And from his average visage, confidence did ooze
From the curls upon his head to his fake Italian shoes.

Two hundred eyes were on him as he walked up to a
    blonde,
Two hundred ears were straining to hear how she'd
    respond.
He wavered for a moment as he saw her in the light.
"She's way too drunk," he muttered. "Wouldn't be too fair a
    fight."

He quickly passed her table; his eyes flicked round the room.
He paused for just a second, then his hunt he did resume,
A brunette in the corner looked like she might be the one
That Casey, mighty Casey, would pick up to have some fun.

She sat there in the shadows, then lit up a cigarette.
The flame was like a spotlight; Casey broke into a sweat.
He quickly changed direction, as though it was meant to be.
What in the dark seemed thirty, in the light looked sixty-
    three.

I thought he'd call it quits, but no, Casey was determined—
His eyes blazed like a zealot's in the middle of a sermon.
And then he saw her standing there—the Beatles song come
    true.
Casey now had found his prey—I had the perfect view.

Her eyes shone like two diamonds, and her cheeks were rosy
    fair,
Her lips were quite inviting; blonde and curly was her hair.
With more curves than mountain roads, her lush body was
    divine.
Though I couldn't read his mind, I'm sure Casey thought,
    "She's mine!"

He smoothed his hair and gave a nod, then checked out his
    reflection.
Satisfied with how he looked, he moved in her direction.
Uncoiling like a cobra, he appeared right at her side.
Oh, he was in his element, and wouldn't be denied.

He started off by asking, "Tell me, is this seat here free?"
Before there was an answer, he plunked down rapidly.
He sat there for a moment, then he ordered up a drink,
Then Casey, mighty Casey, glanced at me and gave a wink.

He leaned upon his elbow, not quite looking at his prey,
Joking with the barkeep, overtipping all the way.
His eyes then locked upon her, and he gave a little start
As though he had just noticed her, whose beauty stole his
    heart.

He started with some small talk, in his soothing sexy voice.
She looked like she might weaken. Did she really have a
    choice?
Then slowly she leaned forward, whispered to this ladies'
    man:
"Ain't never gonna happen, guy, 'cause I'm a huge Leafs fan."

Oh, somewhere in this favoured land the bars now have last
    call;
Guys and girls have hooked up, with each other are
    enthralled,
And somewhere men are laughing, and somewhere children
    shout;
**But there is no joy in Mudville—mighty Casey has struck
    out.**

The Nineteen Hundred and Eighty-Fourth

INSPIRED BY GEORGE ORWELL'S
NINETEEN EIGHTY-FOUR

It was a bright cold day in April, and the clocks were striking thirteen. Tyro Tinnywinkle looked up from his roasted wanbuck sandwich and sighed. Ever since King Fairdwych had declared a twenty-six-hour day to increase productivity, thirteen o'clock had been a symbol of gloom. In fact, the general consensus around Tarnez (the once-proud capital city of the Great Continent of Geologa) was that pretty much *any* o'clock was a symbol of doom now that Fairdwych was king. Tyro usually paid no heed to the affairs conducted within Castle Hardstock, mostly because the affairs conducted within Castle Hardstock never paid heed to him, but this latest decree was hard to ignore. King Fairdwych showed little interest in the health and happiness of his subjects, and everyone in the kingdom knew it.

But there had been a time, not so long ago, when the lives of the royal family and the Tinnywinkle family had been intricately entwined. Sardoz the Curious, Fairdwych's father, spent hours browsing the dusty shelves and bins of what many considered to be the most complete and well-stocked magic shop in the world, Tinnywinkle's House of Magic and Mystical Oddities. And he always bought something: the Canine Bisecting Trick Apparatus, the Mesmerizing Orb of Thallos, or even just a box of itching powder. (The former king wasn't one of those canker-bottoms who browsed in a store, asked for a clerk's recommendations, talked to him for an hour, and then said he had to talk it over with his wife.)

The connection between the royal family and the Tinnywinkle family went even further back. In fact, for as long as the Tinnywinkle family had lived on the Great

Continent of Geologa, they had literally dwelled in the shadow of Castle Hardstock. After it had been damaged in the War of the Clinking Sparrows, Tyro's grandfather had been one of the builders who restored it to its soaring splendour, fortifying its ramparts and getting plastered under its flying buttresses. (Tyro's grandfather became the black sheep of the family when he eschewed a career in magic for the construction business.)

That had been then. These days, the royal family completely ignored the Tinnywinkles. Though, Tyro had to admit, it was hard *not* to be involved with the machinations of ambition, greed, and murder that passed as governance these days. For instance, Fairdwych had recently imposed a tax on everyone taller than himself. At six-foot-four, and still growing (as any respectable twenty-eight-year-old Tarnezian would do), Tyro towered a full eleven inches over the King. That meant the royal coffers were padded an extra eleven hundred guildenfeathers a year from Tyro's own threadbare pocket. The King was a preening, officious, egomaniacal idiot, thought Tyro as he munched his wanbuck deluxe, and Tyro's opinion of the reigning monarch was one of the nicer ones in the kingdom.

King Fairdwych had the distinction of being the first universally hated monarch in Geologa's history. Visit any county, province, or state of the Great Continent and ask, "Who rules this land?" The answer would be "Fairdwych the Hated," or "Fairdwych the Thoroughly Despised," or "That Tiny Bastard King." In neighbouring kingdoms it was rumoured that Fairdwych's subjects took an instant dislike to him just to save time.

Fairdwych had usurped the throne from his brother, the

much-loved Malki the Cross-Eyed, who had been captured by their third cousin Flabym the Witherer during the Cumin Wars. Fairdwych's stepbrother Gandwar, the One With No Nickname, who had also been in line for the throne, had been sent to the Barren Fields of Slowdeath to fight their uncle, Peptor of the Rangollians, to gain an alliance with Buppquar the Belligerent, who had strong trade relations with the Aero peoples and the Binnywhacketorians, both of whom were needed to cement the relationship with the Upper Boodlebears. After that, it got fairly complicated.

'Twas a tangled web of family allegiances and rivalries that trapped the poor inhabitants of Geologa under the tyrannical rule of Fairdwych, That Tiny Bastard King. It was Tyro's belief that there was only one of the whole bunch who could competently rule, and that was Madwyn, sister to Fairdwych and Malki. She too was said to covet the throne, but had disappeared after the Actor Uprising, when all who were involved in the arts protested the lack of funding and respect they received. (Due to a short rehearsal period, the uprising was quelled in an hour and twenty-three minutes.) It was rumoured that Madwyn was now touring with an interpretive dance group. And in fact, Tyro thought he had glimpsed Madwyn at a performance in the town square not too long ago. If it had been her, Tyro reckoned, remembering her lovely eyes and direct manner, she was beautiful *and* brave, for Fairdwych would never allow the return of a sister who could challenge his right to the throne.

Tyro's reverie was interrupted by a kerfuffle outside. He ran to the window of the shop. Adam Two-Blow, the most accomplished kerfuffle player in the land, was playing "The Rise of the Rebels." Tyro cringed because (a) public kerfuffle music had been recently banned by Fairdwych, (b) "The Rise of the Rebels" was always used to incite violence against tyranny, and (c) Tyro hated violence *and* tyranny. Violence and tyranny resulted in danger, and Tyro was not a friend to danger. He wasn't even a casual acquaintance. He tried to avoid danger at all times. He was no coward—he truly wasn't—he just didn't like being bothered.

Tyro stepped back from the window, hoping no one had noticed his interest in the kerfuffle, when the door of Tinnywinkle's House of Magic and Mystical Oddities slammed open and a pair of Siamese twins, each brandishing a broadsword, blustered in.

By the eyes of Lumptor, Tyro thought sourly, I believe I'm about to be bothered.

"Big Brother, did we lose the jackals?" the slightly smaller of the twins gasped, twisting awkwardly to look at his mate.

"I believe so, Little Brother, I believe so. Their blades shall not taste our flesh today!"

Tyro couldn't help but stare. The brothers were strapping specimens, broad shouldered and muscular, with large, fine heads devoid of hair. Except for the fact that they were attached, the left buttock of one to the right buttock of the other, and could never truly stand side by side, they looked as any other pair of twin brothers might.

Little Brother motioned to Tyro. "Big Brother, cast your eyes on yon merchant."

Big Brother turned to look at Tyro, forcing Little Brother to face the door and almost injure himself on the doorknob. "You! Are you Tyro Tinnywinkle?"

"Yes, yes I am. And how can I help you gentlemen today? Some itching powder, perhaps, or our most popular item? Mystical Trick of the Fish?"

"Do not waste your silver tongue on us, Merchant Tinnywinkle. We wish not to purchase your wares. You must depart with us now! There is no time to waste with explanations! The future of Geologa depends on you and you alone!"

Tyro stared. Except for his tendency to constantly exclaim, Big Brother seemed a reasonable fellow. But the future of Geologa depending on Tyro Tinnywinkle, seller of toys and tricks? It strained credulity. No, it was insane. Tyro cleared his throat. "Gentlemen, I think there may have been some mistake. You see——"

With an upward jab of his broadsword, Little Brother spun himself to face Tyro. (Big Brother was wrenched around to face the window, getting slightly tangled in the curtain for a moment.) "There is no mistake. The Oracle has spoken. You are the One."

Tyro cleared his throat to address the small one. "Please don't think I'm not flattered. I am. But——"

For the second time that day, the door of Tinnywinkle's House of Magic and Mystical Oddities slammed open. This time, four of the King's Guards in bright purple livery burst through the door. The largest of the group, bedecked in ribbons and medals that proclaimed his status as leader, sneered. "Kill them all!"

"Excuse me," Tyro said with a nervous chuckle. "There seem to be a lot of mistakes being made today. I am but a simple——"

Tyro's words were drowned out by the battle cry of the brothers. "By the Power of Aphrodesia!"

The brothers rushed at the King's Guards. They moved remarkably quickly and gracefully considering their disadvantage. They were as fast on their feet moving forward or backward, and they seemed to have an almost telepathic knowledge of how the other would move. They spun like a child's top, striking out with their swords, whirling like dervishes, cutting a bloody swath. Three of the King's Guards tried to surround the brothers as the fourth moved menacingly towards Tyro.

"Wait! Wait! I am sure we can talk this over and come to a peaceful resolution."

"Aye, boy, it *will* be peaceful once I cut out your treasonous tongue, remove your head from your body, and crush your still-beating heart!"

Around the "I cut out your treasonous tongue" part, Tyro decided words were not going to help his case. He glanced around for a weapon. Not surprisingly, weapons were in short supply in a magic shop. He picked up what was left of his sandwich and held it in front of him.

The guardsman howled with laughter. "By the Gods of Barmalon! How will I fight this demon, armed with his lunch? I can only pray he does not have a flagon of ale!"

Tyro separated the two pieces of bread and watched as the wanbuck meat fell to his feet. (The guard also watched, puzzled.) While he was distracted, Tyro leapt at him, pressing the two pieces of bread to the huge guardsman's eyes. The guardsman screamed.

Tyro could not have his wanbuck deluxe without adding Tafaleno Lava Sauce. It was a condiment that few could consume without experiencing cramps and painful bowel movements. But it didn't affect Tyro at all. He liked it. Having it rubbed in your eyes, however, was bound to be painful. As the guardsman wept and thrashed around blindly, Tyro picked up a large piece of wood and clocked him on the noggin. The guard crumpled in a heap at Tyro's feet.

"Well done, Tyro!"

Tyro turned to see Little Brother grinning at him (and Big Brother raising his fist in solidarity over Little Brother's shoulder). At their feet lay the remains of the King's Guards.

"Come!" said Big Brother, motioning towards the door. "There will be others who wish to stop us from our quest! To our transport!"

The brothers left Tinnywinkle's House of Magic and Mystical Oddities. Tyro grabbed his coat and man-sack and quickly followed. He knew that the death of four of the King's Guards in his shop would label him a traitor and a murderer, so he went with the brothers. He had a feeling this was to be the start of a great adventure.

Adventures were the only thing Tyro hated more than being bothered.

They had been riding for almost an hour through mountains and valleys. The brothers were up front leading the way, and Tyro brought up the rear. Big Brother rode facing forward, and Little Brother faced backward. Occasionally, he waved back at Tyro, who was clearly enjoying wanbuck riding. Mostly, though, Little Brother kept his eyes peeled for pursuers in the gloomy landscape.

Tyro had been but a small child the last time he had sat astride one of the great beasts. The wanbuck on which the brothers were riding was larger than his, since its load was bigger. Tyro's wanbuck was slightly smaller, but it was a rich scarlet colour that was quite striking. Tyro patted its huge head affectionately.

Wanbucks were exceptional creatures. Larger than plough horses, with feline heads and long, silky ears, they were invaluable in every way imaginable. They had eight legs, but they used only four at a time. They tucked the others in at their sides. When they started to tire, they switched legs. Wanbucks could run non-stop for up to three days. The back four legs were stronger than the front four and allowed the wanbuck to leap to a height of almost sixty feet. Their skin was thick enough to withstand any direct hit by an arrow, but soft enough to line a pillow. But the most remarkable thing of all was that all wanbucks knew, *instinctually*, when they were going to die. They would then travel to the nearest butcher, lie down, and expire. Their body they offered up as a final gift, and every part was delicious.

The group had been riding for almost four hours when Tyro grew weary. As the keeper of a magic shop, he was not accustomed to long rides, or saddle sores.

"Um," Tyro called, "where are we going?"

"To the Forest of Deepening Despair, my friend," replied Little Brother. "There we will meet the rest of our allies."

"*The Forest of Deepening Despair?* I look forward to it. Is the Valley of Approaching Death all booked up?"

The brothers laughed as one.

"You amuse us, shopkeeper!" shouted Big Brother. "My brother and I enjoy laughing. Many's a time we trade quips as our cold steel dispatches our enemies."

"Um, yes, always nice to laugh," Tyro mumbled. "So, we get to the forest, then what?"

"Then you will tell us how to defeat the King," said Little Brother matter-of-factly.

Tyro stared at Little Brother. "Hmm. Interesting. I am fairly certain I have no idea how to defeat the King. I am certain, because even now as I speak, thoughts are racing through my head and not one of them is labelled *How to Defeat the King*."

"The Oracle is never wrong," called Big Brother over his shoulder. "She has been blessed with a power that none of us will ever understand."

"What exactly did she say?" asked Tyro.

Little Brother closed his eyes and intoned with great seriousness: "The One upon whom success does rely shall declare with words of little import that which is most important. For a quest to succeed, the One shall go beyond his station and do what none have done before him." Little Brother opened his eyes and crossed his arms. He looked at Tyro meaningfully.

"What does that even mean? Why do oracles have to be so mysterious? Why don't they just say, 'The King is taking a walk alone in the garden at 2:25 P.M. Stick a sword in him, then run away'? But nooo, oracles have to be vague. That prediction could be about anyone or anything. There is nothing the Oracle said that pertains specifically to me."

"The Oracle said the One is named Tyro Tinnywinkle, the magic seller."

Tyro was silent for a moment. "I have to admit that does seem more specific."

Twenty minutes later the brothers and Tyro were in the heart of the Forest of Deepening Despair. The forest was quite lovely, filled as it was with soft mosses, golden leaves, and sweet birdsong.

"I have to say," said Tyro, "the Forest of Deepening Despair is not living up to its name."

The brothers guffawed.

"The forest was named by the mistress of King Ratnor the Vertical. She was bipolar," explained Big Brother. "Many places with fearsome names amount to nothing," he added.

Little Brother agreed. "'Tis the sweet names that you should worry about. Makes you let your guard down. I could tell you tales that would curdle your very blood. About places that the Devil himself would think twice about setting foot in. The Valley of the Returning Lamb, Baby Bumpkin's Point, the Cave of Lingering Passion."

Big Brother shivered. Tyro shivered just to see that something could make Big Brother shiver. These lads had not seemed to fear anything.

"Stop here." Little Brother jumped off the wanbuck, pulling along his brother, who was ready for the quick dismount.

As Tyro looked around, all manner of Tarnezians crept out of the woods. They dropped from branches, parted bushes, and emerged from beneath piles of golden leaves. Soon, the brothers and Tyro were surrounded.

Big Brother addressed the crowd. "My friends! May I present Tyro Tinnywinkle. The One who will lead us to victory!"

The crowd burst into enthusiastic cheers.

Tyro burst into enthusiastic dread.

Big and Little Brother led Tyro and the rest of the group—well, *deeper* into the Forest of Deepening Despair. In Tyro's mind, at least, it was starting to live up to its name. Barely any sun at all filtered through the dense leaves here, and the mossy forest floor gave way to naked rocks, broken sticks, and mud. Mosquitoes buzzed about the wanbucks, and they swished their tails to repel them.

How did I get involved in this? Tyro wondered, ducking a low-hanging branch. I'm a *shopkeeper*. I am not equipped to face warfare, sacrifice, and hardship. And I certainly don't have the wherewithal to lead a rebel army to victory—unless that army is fighting bored ten-year-olds at a birthday party—but even then, the odds would be sixty–forty on the children.

The group entered a large clearing festooned with perhaps a hundred, two hundred tents.

"How many people are there here?" Tyro asked.

Little Brother's chest swelled with pride. "We have nineteen hundred and eighty-three brave souls who have joined us in our hope for a better tomorrow."

"Impressive," admitted Tyro. "But you're still out-numbered by the King's Guard."

The brothers laughed and slapped the hapless merchant on the back in unison.

"By the Hair of Hecubah!" said Big Brother. "You are a veritable Gus of Gloom! And anyway, the odds are a little better now, for you are the *nineteen hundred and eighty-fourth*." Bugles sounded in the distance.

"Come," said Little Brother, with a laugh. "You must meet the Queen."

"The Queen? We have no queen."

Big Brother scowled at Tyro. "Not at this precise moment, no. But tomorrow ... that is a different thing altogether."

They were now standing in front of a huge tent stitched together with swaths of crimson and emerald and turquoise fabrics. Its doorway was guarded by two of the largest men Tyro had ever seen.

Big Brother nodded to them. "Francis, Periwinkle. We wish an audience with the Queen."

The one named Francis nodded back. His black, blazing eyes bored through Tyro. "She is waiting for you. Enter."

They entered.

The inside of the tent was even grander than the outside. It was hung with antique lamps that cast a rosy glow over banquet tables overflowing with bottles of wine, platters of fruit, loaves of bread, and wedges of very stinky cheese. The tent could comfortably sleep a couple of hundred people, Tyro thought. About eight hundred uncomfortably.

The brothers and he were led to the end of the tent, where sat the most beautiful woman Tyro had ever seen. His mouth dropped open.

The brothers bowed their heads and knelt down. "Your Majesty," they whispered in unison.

Tyro broke out of his reverie and noticed the brothers on their knees. He knelt just as they stood up.

"Queen Madwyn, may we present Tyro Tinnywinkle."

"Please rise, Tyro."

Tyro stood and tried to restrain himself from openly staring at this vision before him. The beauty of her face was unsettling enough, but when paired with the overwhelming aura of kindness and love that enveloped her, Tyro actually grew faint.

"So, you are the One who will restore me to the throne?"

"Uh … I will certainly try, my Majesty … Your Majestic … Queen … My Queen." Tyro bowed deeply, and the blood rushed back to his head.

"Please call me Madwyn. We don't stand on ceremony here." She turned her attention to the brothers. "How was everything in town?"

Little Brother frowned. "The people are giving up hope. They wish to see you on the throne, Majesty, but many believe you to be dead. Even more fear openly defying the hated Fairdwych. For his armies fight to the death, no matter what the personal cost."

Madwyn's slate-grey eyes turned cold. "I will never forgive my brother for what he has done to our land. Never."

Big Brother cleared his throat. "It gets worse. Fairdwych has scheduled a Mystic Crowning ceremony for tomorrow evening."

"What's a Mystic Crowning ceremony?" asked Tyro.

"Tomorrow?" Madwyn jumped up from her seat. "If he conjures up Tarmanock, all is lost! We must move up our attack!"

"What's Tarmanock?" Tyro asked. "Is it bad? Is it part of the Mystic Crowning?"

"Could we be ready for tomorrow morning?" Madwyn asked the brothers.

"Is this crowning thing very dangerous? Is it something we really have to worry about? I mean, could we just not show up? It seems rude without an invitation or a—"

The brothers smiled at their Queen. "We have been ready for months, Majesty. We shall solidify our plans and, with Tyro here, make our way to success." Big Brother slapped Tyro on the back.

Tyro looked at the Queen. "Yes. About that. First, I guess the whole Mystic Crowning information will be given to me later. Not important, really. Just like to know if I need to bring a gift. Here is my concern, and I have no wish to disrespect your Oracle, but I really have no idea what's going on here, and I need to get back to the shop and close up."

Madwyn smiled beneficently. "Do not let worry furrow your brow, Tyro. The Oracle spoke. You will lead us to where we must go."

The brothers grabbed Tyro by the shoulders. "To the War Tent, young Tyro."

Tyro had just enough time to give a hasty nod and curtsy to the Queen before he was hurried out of her presence.

"Listen, fellows," Tyro said as he was ushered from the big tent. "I really don't know how I can help."

The brothers looked at each other, then at Tyro.

Big Brother spoke cryptically: "Then let the Fates have their way with all."

Tyro raised his finger in question, then lowered it when Big Brother frowned.

In the War Tent, the brothers and the leaders of the rebel squadrons pored over a blueprint of Castle Hardstock. Big Brother went into the plan.

"As you can see, the walls are heavily fortified. Not even cannon fire can pierce them. There is but one way in. We will have a diversion at the east wall here." Big Brother pointed at the blueprint.

Little Brother continued. "While the King's Guard is dealing with that, we have one hundred and twenty of our best warriors on wanbucks on the northwest wall. It is the lowest of the walls, and the wanbucks should be able to clear it easily. Our warriors will have to hold that position until the wanbucks can jump back and return with more reinforcements. At the same time, our archers will lead an attack on the south wall"—Little Brother pointed to another spot on the map—"and add additional support for the northwest wall."

Big Brother looked pained. "We will lose many good men and women, but if we can gain control of the courtyard, we can bring the Queen in, place her on the throne, and stop the Mystic Crowning ceremony."

Tyro cleared his throat. "I'm not sure, but I may have asked this before. What is the Mystic Crowning ceremony?"

Big Brother craned his neck around and nodded to Little Brother. Little Brother turned to Tyro and steepled his fingers.

"As you may know, the royal family has long been intrigued by the magical arts. Fairdwych has taken that passion beyond all reasoning. He found, in his father's library, a book of demonic spells. In it, he discovered the

Mystic Crowning ceremony, which can only be performed every three thousand and forty-three years during the Day of the Sixteen Whirlers. Tomorrow is that day. "

Big Brother continued. "If the ceremony is carried out, a demon called Tarmanock will be called forth and will pledge undying allegiance to the one who released him. This beast has *ungodly* power, and with it Fairdwych will never be stopped."

Tyro felt faint. "How is it that I never knew of this book of demonic spells?"

Big Brother patted his back. "It was long thought to be a hoax till one of our spies saw Fairdwych using a spell from it to ... discipline the kitchen help."

Tyro's throat dried. "I don't want to know the details, do I?"

Little Brother shook his head. "No, you most certainly do not."

Tyro wondered aloud: "Is there any chance Tarmanock will be like the rest of us and take an instant dislike to the King? Maybe he'll kill him and head back to his own dimension."

The brothers looked at him sadly and shook their heads. Tyro sighed and rubbed his temples. He looked at the blueprints of the castle. Something caught his eye.

"Wait a minute. This blueprint doesn't show the tunnel."

All eyes turned to him.

"Tunnel?" said Big Brother.

"There's a tunnel that starts by the River of Lost Tears and leads straight into the castle. My grandfather was one of the engineers. He showed it to me when I was a child. Used to play in it for hours. Can't remember why we stopped."

"There's a tunnel?" Little Brother exclaimed. "Our army can enter the castle undetected via this old tunnel?"

The group laughed delightedly. There was much handshaking and backslapping. Big Brother wiped happy tears from his eyes.

"So was that it?" Tyro asked hopefully. "Am I done?"

Everyone laughed harder.

The next morning, as the brothers prepared to lead their assembled men to the head of the tunnel, Madwyn approached Tyro.

"Tyro, I thank you for your service. We are fortunate indeed to have your help. The Fates have been kind to deliver you to us."

"But I haven't done anything, Majesty, except remember a treasured childhood haunt."

"Ah, but this tunnel allows us access to the castle in such a way that will save many lives." Madwyn paused, looking into Tyro's eyes. "Is everything all right?"

Everything was fine. Tyro could not help staring at Madwyn. He had never seen anyone so beautiful before.

"Yes, Majesty. Everything is fine, thank you. I was just thinking of ... a favourite recipe ... that I like ... um ... I hope you get the throne. I always liked you best."

"Thank you." Madwyn smiled sadly. "I hope that I can get it back, too. My brother has almost broken the spirit of our country with his greed and lust for power."

"Yes, well, family can be complex."

"There's nothing complex about Fairdwych. He will

try to separate my head from my body if he sees me and figures out what we're up to."

"I will not let that happen, Your Queenship ... my Queen ... Your Majesty." Tyro blushed.

"Call me Madwyn. 'Tis my name." She laughed softly and kissed Tyro on the cheek. "Good luck to you today. May we all survive."

Tyro was so besotted by the kiss, it took him a few seconds to understand the import of her words. "Good luck to me? Why? I thought I was done. What am I doing that I might not survive?"

What Tyro was doing was leading an army of rebels to the River of Lost Tears. As they rode up to the mouth of the tunnel, Tyro turned to the brothers. "There you go. That's the tunnel. Leads right into the main ballroom, right next to the Throne Room."

"Excellently done, my friend!" said Big Brother. "Now you must lead us to the end."

"What? I've led you to where you want to go! What else do you need me for? I'm not a warrior."

"You are still an important part of this." Madwyn rode up next to him with an old woman by her side.

"This is the Oracle." Madwyn gestured to the old woman. "She foretold of you. She says there is more that you must do."

Tyro looked narrowly at the Oracle, despising her more than anyone he had ever despised.

"Okay, Oracle. What am I to do next?"

"I do not know," the Oracle intoned sagely.

"You have no idea?"

"I would not want to say," she pronounced regally.

"So, I'm to lead an army of rebels to take the throne from the King and defeat his army because—you just had a *feeling*?"

"I am the Oracle! My prognostications have changed all that we know!" The old woman sounded testy.

"Will I live through this?" Tyro asked hopefully.

"I don't know."

"Will we succeed today?"

"The immediate future is cloudy."

"What's my favourite colour?"

"Blue."

"Lucky guess."

"The Oracle has correctly foretold Tyro's favourite colour!" Big Brother shouted triumphantly. The rebels cheered.

"That doesn't mean anything!" cried Tyro. He turned back to the Oracle. "How accurate are your feelings? What percentage would you say?"

"That is not important now, young Tyro. You have brought us here. As I have foretold. You have completed the first of your tasks."

"My *tasks*? Tasks, as in more than one? What are they?"

"What is known to you is known to me, but what is known to me has yet to be known to you," she croaked.

"So, what you are saying is, you don't know anything."

Madwyn raised her delicate eyebrows. "Is there something wrong, Tyro? Are you having second thoughts about securing the throne for me?"

"No," said Tyro quickly. "Just going over my tasks." He turned to the rebel army and in his best military style shouted, "Let's move out!"

Tyro led the rebel group into the mouth of the tunnel. It had a dank odour (as one would expect from a tunnel), but the phosphorus that lined its walls provided enough light to see by. Tyro was thinking back to the last time he had been here. He'd played in that nook there, had hidden by this cranny here, had stowed his little treasure of bobbins and sticks in that hole way up there. As he looked around he was overcome by a wave of nostalgia. Why do we have to grow up? he wondered. As he followed a smooth, familiar curve in the tunnel, he saw a huge shadow about five hundred feet ahead.

Tyro raised his hand to stop the crowd behind him. He whispered loudly, in a rising panic: "I remember why this tunnel isn't used anymore."

"What is it, friend?" asked Big Brother.

"A Twavverhackle!"

The entire group took a giant involuntary step back. The Twavverhackle was the most fearsome creature in Geologa. The very name would put misbehaving children on the straight and narrow, and frustrated parents invoked its fearsomeness only rarely. It scared them too.

Hundreds of Twavverhackles had roamed the countryside in days gone by, but they had all mysteriously disappeared about twenty years ago. Since they were impossible to kill, it was thought that they had become extinct due to some strange evolutionary weakness.

Unfortunately, no one had told the Twavverhackle who was now blocking their path. This one looked extremely lively and appeared to be a prime example of the species. It towered sixty feet high and looked like the offspring of an alligator and a great ape. The only thing worse than its huge jaws was its proclivity for hurling its own feces.

"This is going to be a bit of a problem," said Big Brother, unsheathing his broadsword.

"You mean the sixty-foot creature that wants to kill us?" said Tyro. "Yes, I fully agree with you."

Little Brother cut him off. "No time for sarcasm, little one."

"Oh no, what do *you* want?" Tyro asked as the Oracle approached.

"You will get us past the creature."

Tyro laughed. "Have I done something to you, *personally*? Why are you so hell-bent on getting me killed?"

"You are wrong, Tyro Tinnywinkle. You will live. You are the key to all success. From the lowly will come all happiness."

"Lowly?"

"Even the smallest rat has its purpose."

"That's sweet."

"Without manure, there can be no—"

"GOT IT!" Tyro yelled. "I think we all have the gist here. I'm lowly and will make all good. Yes, I think that is clear. Here is something else that is clear. There is no way in MARKO'S GREAT CAVERN that I am going back there to face that thing."

"Of course, Tyro, you are under no obligation. You have done what we have asked of you." Tyro turned to see that

Madwyn had joined the group. "If I am to lead, it is up to me to get us past this."

Big Brother spoke up. "My Queen, perhaps the original plan of using the wanbucks to—"

"No, Big Brother," Madwyn said firmly. "Going through the tunnel is our best chance for success." She turned to a servant. "Get me my broadsword."

"Wait!" said Tyro. "I'll go." This surprised everyone, especially Tyro. "Look, if the old crone is right, then I will somehow get us past this without getting killed." He looked at the Oracle. "Are you absolutely certain about this?"

"Seventy percent certain. Maybe seventy-three."

Tyro's jaw dropped. "Seventy-three percent?"

"That is still quite favourable odds."

"A hundred percent is quite favourable. Seventy percent leaves a lot of room for disaster."

Big Brother and Little Brother clasped him by the shoulders.

"We shall come with you, friend," said Big Brother, puffing out his chest.

"May the Fates be kind," said Little Brother.

Tears sprang into Tyro's eyes. "That is very nice of you. No one has ever looked out for me like this. No." He snuffled. "I will go by myself and take care of the Twavverhackle."

The Oracle smiled. "I knew you would."

Tyro had never wanted to punch someone more. He buttoned up his coat.

"Are you sure this is all you will need?" asked Big Brother.

"I'm not actually sure of anything," said Tyro, rolling up his sleeves. "Except that our weapons are useless against the Twavverhackle. Perhaps I can scare it off with a flash strip or a very impressive card trick."

"Good luck to you," said Little Brother. "May the Harbinger of Death pass you by today!"

"Thanks." Tyro slowly made his way forward to where the Twavverhackle lay in wait. He had no plan, no weapons, no chance of surviving. Exactly why I hate adventures, he thought bitterly.

He moved farther into the tunnel, staying close to the wall, hoping to blend in with the shadows. He took a glance around the curved wall. There was no sign of the Twavverhackle. Odd, he thought, it's very difficult for a sixty-foot creature to be inconspicuous. Tyro moved even deeper into the tunnel. As he reached a precariously rocky part, the Twavverhackle leapt out, roaring ferociously. It was the most terrifying sound Tyro had ever heard. What happened next happened so quickly that Tyro barely had time to register the events. But register them he did.

Tyro raised his hands to protect himself.

As he raised his hands, he released the two dovelings that were secreted in his coat, two dovelings he had counted during inventory check at the shop the night before.

The dovelings, excited at being freed from the confines of the coat, sang lustily and flew right at the Twavverhackle's beady eyes.

The only thing a Twavverhackle fears, for reasons known only to it, is a doveling. The only thing a Twavverhackle fears more than one doveling is two. Two dovelings were too much to bear for the Twavverhackle, who immediately had a heart attack and died.

Tyro stood over the dead Twavverhackle. "That was

easy." He turned and yelled down the tunnel. "You can all come back now! The creature is dead! I killed it."

A loud cheer echoed through the tunnel.

Fifteen minutes later, the rebel army was almost at its destination. The constant questioning of the Brothers about the demise of the Twavverhackle made it seem to Tyro as if three times that amount of time had passed.

"Did you jump on its back and twist its neck until it broke?" asked Little Brother as he ran up with Big Brother.

"No. Of course, that was my first thought, but, uh, it's not important how I did it. Ah, here we are."

They had reached the end.

The brothers, Tyro, Madwyn, and the Oracle stood at the secret door that led into the ballroom. Tyro stuck a cautious head in. The magnificently opulent ballroom glistened with golden chandeliers, long tables covered with elaborately decorated silver tablecloths, and several life-size statues of Fairdwych.

"There's no one about," Madwyn whispered to the squadron leaders. "Bring your people in, quietly. Brothers, Tyro, you will come with me. You too, Mavellus." She gestured to the leader of the archers. "Those stairs lead to the level above the Throne Room where the advisers to the monarch and the people's representatives sit. That is, until my brother disbanded them. Three hundred of your archers can easily stand there. We shall surround the King and his guards. Hopefully, they will see the folly in resistance and we can end this without any blood being spilled. May the Gods be with you all."

Madwyn led the way up the stairs.

Tyro marvelled at how three hundred archers could

move so quietly up uncarpeted stairs. Five minutes later everyone was in place above the throne of Fairdwych the Despised. Madwyn and Tyro peeked over the banister and glanced at the scene below. One hundred Royal Guards were preparing for what Tyro assumed was the Mystic Crowning. Large orbs were set in the shape of a pentagram, and herbs smoked in pots around the perimeter. A very nervous goat bleated from her place in the centre. Fairdwych appeared to be in an impatient mood.

Pointing at the workers with his sceptre, he screamed, "Move faster, you square-headed buffoons! The time of the Mystic Crowning is almost upon us! We must be ready. Then the world will be mine! *Mine alone!*"

I really hate that guy, thought Tyro.

Madwyn turned to make sure the archers were in place. They were. She stood up, looking every inch the Queen she was. "Fairdwych! This stops now!"

Startled, Fairdwych looked up. When he saw her, he smiled. "Sister! How lovely to see you. I thought we would never cross paths again. How can I help you?"

"It is I who will help you, Brother. I will help you step down as ruler and live a life away from here, where you can cause no harm."

Fairdwych smiled again.

A chill ran up Tyro's spine.

Something was not right here.

"Sister, tell your archers to put down their weapons."

Tyro saw Madwyn begin to falter.

"Archers ... put ... down ..." She seemed to be having trouble speaking.

"Madwyn! What are you doing?" Tyro saw that the

archers seemed to be in the same state as their Queen. They started to lower their bows. What was going on?

"Sister! You can't resist me. You should know that. Put down your weapons and I'll make sure your death is a quick one."

Tyro started to feel light-headed himself. As if his will was being slowly eroded. He looked closely at the sceptre Fairdwych clutched. Of course! On top of it was the Mesmerizing Orb of Thallos! A mystical talisman that his grandfather accidentally sold to King Sardoz. It had the power to make all within its vicinity the pawns of the possessor. Tyro fought its influence. Years of magic shows and dealing with disgruntled hypnotists had given him a slight edge in overcoming the power of the orb, but even so, he knew he would succumb eventually. Quickly, he reached for the nearest archer's bow. He placed an arrow against the taut twine, aimed at the orb, and pulled back.

"You will not win, tyrant!" Tyro loosed his arrow. It sliced through the air and glanced off the backside of the goat, ricocheting off one of the herb pots and fraying the goat's tether. The panicked goat strained against her bond.

"Fool!" Fairdwych shouted. "Why do you try to kill my goat?"

"I'm not trying to kill the— Oh, blast it!"

Tyro grabbed another arrow, took aim, and shot a portrait of the despised King.

"Stop this minute! That was my favourite painting!" Fairdwych shook his fist at Tyro.

The goat broke free of her rope and did what every

living creature that encountered Fairdwych wanted to do. Attacked him *viciously*. The goat butted Fairdwych in the stomach, which caused him to loosen his grip on the sceptre. It fell to the ground, shattering the orb into a million pieces.

As though awakening from a deep sleep, Madwyn, the brothers, the archers, and all the King's men came to their senses.

Madwyn was the first to fully regain her wits. "Grab him! Grab the pretender to the throne. As your Queen, I command you!"

As the guards started to surround him, Fairdwych screamed: "I may not be the ruler of Geologa. But neither shall you be, Sister!" With that, he took a knife from his robe and hurled it at Madwyn.

Everyone stood in shock, except for Tyro. He jumped in front of Madwyn, and the knife hit him squarely in the chest. The brothers gasped.

Fortunately it was the handle of the knife that hit Tyro. (Fairdwych was not an expert in the art of knife throwing.) Guards grabbed the disgraced and despised King and took him away.

Madwyn hugged Tyro tightly. "You saved my life!"

"No, I saved you from a bruise. Your brother throws like a girl."

Madwyn picked up the knife and threw it at the coat of arms on the back of the throne, where it lodged itself perfectly.

"He doesn't throw like this girl."

Madwyn then kissed Tyro passionately. The best, most

glorious kiss ever.

When his breath returned, Tyro asked, "Are you allowed to do that? I mean … I'm just a commoner."

Madwyn smiled. "I can do whatever I want. I'm the Queen." She kissed him again.

The Oracle smiled too. "I knew that would happen."

The party spread from inside Castle Hardstock to the capital city of Tarnez below, to the entire continent of Geologa. All were ecstatic at this glorious turn of events and all knew deep within their hearts that this was the beginning of a new golden age.

Big and Little Brother, having consumed a large amount of ale, were in a bit of a melancholy state.

"What do we do now, Big Brother? No more thrones to save, no more tyranny to overcome."

"There will always be a need for warriors such as us," said Big Brother reassuringly. "That is the world's curse and it is our gift." He smiled. "I must say I am impressed with young Tyro. As brave as we, but with none of our skills. Yet he led us to the tunnel, killed a Twavverhackle, and wounded a goat. I'm glad he found it within himself to help the country that gives him his home."

"Yes," said Little Brother. "Though I do not believe that he did what he did out of any patriotic feeling. Are you blind, Big Brother? Did you not notice how he looked at our new Queen from the very first time that he saw her? Tyro did all of this because he loves Madwyn. It's just that simple. **He loved, Big Brother.**"

A Tale of Two Critters

INSPIRED BY CHARLES DICKENS'S
A TALE OF TWO CITIES

It was the best of times, it was the worst of times, it was the age of wisdom, it was the age of foolishness, it was the epoch of belief, it was the epoch of incredulity, it was the season of Light, it was the season of Darkness, it was the spring of hope, it was the winter of despair, we had everything before us, we had nothing before us, we were all going direct to Heaven, we were all going direct the other way. To be more specific, it was Tuesday.

Every momentous occasion of my life seems to have occurred on a Tuesday. I was born on a Tuesday. The day I fulfilled my destiny was a Tuesday. And it seems that the day I cease to exist will be a Tuesday. That's today.

Watching those words flow from my pen as I sit in this wretched little cell has quite a surreal aspect. As I write this, I notice every detail of my enclosure, the peeling paint of the walls, the thickness of the bars; I calculate its exact dimensions—wall to wall and floor to window. As my peripheral vision scans over the bed shoved between the wall and toilet, the image sparks a brainstorm. The bedsprings could be converted to … oh, and the sheets! The radio that doesn't work could easily … Yes, yes … carry the nine, and …

Apologies. I didn't mean to write down my thoughts verbatim. One of the problems of being a genius is you can never write as fast as you think. Just *one* of the problems, as you will soon discover. Shall I opt for a more linear narrative and begin at the beginning? I want to get this all down before the end comes.

As with all creatures great and small, I was born. In a cave in the Arizona desert I breathed my first breath and met the world with the cry of my kind. That was the last time that I did anything remotely characteristic of my genus. Within days, the differences that would set me apart from my brothers began to appear. To start, I learned to walk upright on my hind legs. The quizzical looks from my mother and father as I strode forward (quite gracefully in my opinion) quickly gave way to fear and suspicion. When I spoke, it was not the cry or howl of a pup, but the refined intonations of an Oxford don. One day, barely out of my infancy, I awoke to find my parents gone. They left no trace of their habitation and no note explaining their destination. Of course, no note was perfectly understandable. They were coyotes.

As you know, dear reader, coyotes have no concept of composing or of writing. (A quick glance at the list of every writer that ever lived would show that not one was a coyote.) Of course, there are a multitude of reasons for this. Coyotes have no opposable thumbs. Their artistic instincts are next to nil. They are consumed with the business of being coyotes. They hunt, they eat, they sleep.

They yip-yip-yip at the moon. That is the life of the coyote, the life my parents led. I often pitied them, although if I am being completely honest, just as often I envied them their simplicity.

I have no idea why I am the way I am. My genus is *Canis latrans,* but my *genius* … ah, that is something quite unique. Perhaps my singularity is the result of some highly advanced genetic mutation or perhaps some cruel joke by the Creator. Perhaps my mother ate a bad javelina during my gestational period. Who knows? But I suspect that my mind was so powerful that it willed my body to evolve so I would not follow the path of my parents and forebears. It always seems to come down to dysfunctional families, doesn't it? Not that I ever bore ill will to the ones who sired me. They did the best they could; they were simply not properly equipped. Would things have been different if I were like the others? If I hadn't been born with the IQ of a genius? Yes, I suppose they would.

After my parents left, I tried to embrace the life of the average coyote—for perhaps an hour. It was so boring! Oh look, I'm lazing in the sun. Gee whiz, I'm hunting for food. Hey, I'm lazing in the sun again! Oh boy, it's time for bed. Really? That's living? How do animals do it? It's mind-numbing. I realized then that I could not change what I was. If the life of a coyote wasn't for me, perhaps the life of a more sophisticated vertebrate was. And so I tried to assimilate into human society. As you might imagine, it was disastrous.

Born with a deep love for culture, I was especially drawn to theatre. Shakespeare, Chekov, Shaw—their words drew me into a world I could only dream of inhabiting. I slipped with ease into darkened theatres and playhouses and relished this world of costume and make-believe. It was a world that seemed made for me. And so when I stumbled upon an ad in the *Desert Times* for extras for a film shooting a few miles away, my path grew clear. With the help of a straight razor, a freshly purloined suit, and more than just a little acting talent, I secured the role of Mutant Coyote Man #3 in the exotically titled *Beast Men of Peru*. (The movie, although derivative of many superior horror films, benefits from some sharp performances, first-rate production values, and a script that keeps the genre fresh. But I digress.) I thought living the life of a desert creature was interminable, but it was a circus of fireworks compared to that two-week period. Acting, I soon discovered, was even more boring than hunting for voles all day. And actors! My God! I don't know if all human beings are that self-involved, but if they are, bring on a meteor.

"Oh, I got very close to a Froot Loops commercial."

"Martin Scorsese *nodded* at me after a scene!"

"I'm on the Lipto-Low-Fat-Good-Fat-No-Cholesterol-Suck-on-Leather diet. I've lost a pound and a half of self-loathing."

Hour after hour, day after day, they rambled incessantly about themselves. Rabbit Man #6 was in the middle of a re-enactment of his fourth-place finish on *The Biggest Loser* when I couldn't take it anymore and savaged him. I was fired from the production, but in retrospect, it was all for the best. I really wanted to direct anyway.

So there I was, living between two worlds, a part of neither. But then it happened: a seemingly small event that changed the course of my life forever.

One scorching-hot afternoon, as I wandered through the desert—like Moses, but instead of leading the Israelites, my only followers were three gnats buzzing about my backside and a wasp named Darby—I came across a flyer impaled on a cactus. It was an advertisement for "The Company That Makes Everything" and was looking for beta testers—hardy souls who would try out their mail-order inventions and devices. I was on that job application faster than *Anas platyrhynchos* on *Polyphylla decemlineata*. (For those not up on their binomial nomenclature, I was on it faster than a duck on a June bug. And shame on you for not knowing that! A mind is a terrible thing to waste.)

Within months I was The Company's most prolific tester. I tried out everything from Dehydrated Tyrannosauruses to Solar-Powered Jet Sleds. I often marvelled at the ingenuity of the nameless inventors whose products came to my door. Just as often, I was perplexed. I mean, dehydrated Tyrannosauruses? Really? What possible use would that be to anyone? (Here's a helpful hint: Never carry a box of dehydrated T-rexes in your The Company Sponge Suit during a rainstorm. Trust me.) No matter. I had a job to do and I did it. And I did it brilliantly, I must say. My reports were extremely detailed and I even offered suggestions for improvements. They were all eventually implemented and I received generous royalties. With the money I made, and with the contacts that my brief sojourn in show business brought me, I invested in a couple of blockbuster movies (thank you, *Titanic*), sold some of my simpler patents (ShamWow is mine—no thanks necessary), and within months had a nice little nest egg.

You might think that I was a true success story, that

I would never go hungry again. You might surmise that I could eat in the finest restaurants if I so wished. That would be true if the finest restaurants didn't object to the patronage of a five-foot-six talking coyote. Needless to say, they did object, and quite strenuously, too. So I had to go elsewhere for nourishment. Those frozen Company dinners were delightful, but they didn't always satisfy. And, if I am to be completely truthful, the ancient urge to hunt my food was strong, no matter how civilized I thought I was. In the early days it bothered me that I was at the mercy of a deeply embedded animal instinct found in the simplest of life forms. You can take the coyote out of the desert but you can't change the neural patterns ingrained in the species for millennia. (I realize that last sentence isn't snappy enough to be a bumper sticker, but I'm sure you catch my drift. I needed to hunt.) Voles, prairie dogs, snakes, lizards, even livestock were no match for my lethal combination of savagery and intelligence. Not a single one—until Him.

The first time I laid eyes on Him is as clear in my mind as though it happened yesterday. It was a particularly hot day (I'm fairly sure it was a Tuesday) and hunger gnawed at my belly. I was checking out my usual haunts: Dead Man Boulder Cliff, Steep Fall Peak, Swollen Tongue Creek. All proved fruitless—well, meatless, actually. Suddenly, I caught the scent of something bird*like*, but gamier and with the slightest whiff of ozone. The aroma filled my senses and made me mad with desire. The blood lust was upon me—I imagine it was much like what those handsome vampires in novels go through. (Why are all vampire protagonists incredibly handsome? I'd like to write a book about an ugly, cross-eyed vampire. You, know raise the stakes. Stakes! Being a genius and being funny aren't mutually exclusive, as you see. I know for a fact that Einstein was fond of dumb-blonde jokes.) I was almost painfully overcome with need. I wanted, I *thirsted* for this prey. I truly and completely hungered for Him.

Now, as you are no doubt aware, coyotes hunt in pairs. If you weren't aware, might I suggest catching the Discovery Channel every once in a while? You might learn something. Being an outcast from my species made a partnership impossible, but, up to this point, I had never needed anyone else. When you're a genius, the lower forms tend to get in the way. So, as I had done in all of my previous hunts, I crept slowly along the desert floor following the scent of my prey. I spotted Him pecking at some seed, just off the highway that curved all through our little desert world. (There never seemed to be any traffic on that highway, unless of course I was standing in the middle of it.) There He was—a giant bird. I had never seen one this big before. He was a magnificent specimen: bright blue feathers covered His plump little body, and purple plumage adorned His head. One enormous tail feather completed the ensemble. He looked more ostrich than anything else. Like me, He seemed quite unique.

Excitement filled me to capacity, almost bursting from my pores. I shook with anticipation and every nerve ending pulsated with life. Keeping downwind, I crept forward slowly, patiently, silently until I was within pouncing distance. I stiffened, and with a twitch of my powerful haunches I launched into a beautifully defined arc towards my unsuspecting prey. At the height of my attack, He blinked His obscenely long eyelashes at me, stuck out His tongue, and ran. No, He didn't run—He *exploded* with motion. With a speed that outpaced The Company's Turbo-Charged Rocket Crocs, He disappeared into the horizon, dust clouds billowing in His wake.

Surely my eyes were deceiving me? There was no possible way that He could have travelled so far so fast. I was alternately dumbfounded and enraged. And I have to admit, I was intrigued. Later that day the same thing happened. I spied Him crossing the desert freeway between two enormous boulders. Then: track, sneak, pounce—dust cloud. This time, to add insult to injury (I was agonizingly hungry at this point), He had the audacity to mock me with an inane vocalization that sounded very much like "meep meep." My blood boiled. How could I, a genius, be outwitted by this idiotic bird?

My days and nights were consumed by my efforts to catch Him. I tried every trick I could think of, every manoeuvre imprinted on my hunter's DNA, and yet our battles—if I can call them that—always ended the same way. I landed on my face, He stuck out His tongue, burped a "meep meep," then shook His absurdly perky tail feather in my direction and sped out of sight. He was becoming an obsession to me, but I refused to accept it. I convinced myself He was merely a puzzle that my scientific nature wanted to solve (and my highly evolved gullet wanted to break down in its gastric juices). When solving that puzzle proved difficult, I made up my mind to forgo the ancient hunting strategies of my ancestors and modernize. The Company had a giant catalogue of devices and weapons that would help me in my quest to catch this devil bird.

Looking back, I am amazed at my blindness to two extremely obvious truths. The first was that eating Him was becoming secondary to just wanting to kill the bugger. What exactly would be left to consume if I detonated Him with TNT birdseed? Or the Nitroglycerine Milkshake? The Nuclear Bazooka? I suppose I was more concerned about why these explosive gadgets didn't detonate on cue. How did He escape unharmed every time? Which led me to the second truth I blissfully ignored: What kind of an idiot was I, that it didn't dawn on me that any one of those explosions should have ended my life? How and when did I accept I was immortal? After the exploding X-39 Sled, the TNT Cyborg Doberman, the Giant Boulder Catapult, the Avalanche Simulation Pills, the Bolo Grenade? Every one of those The Company devices malfunctioned. But somehow, through every explosion, every maiming, every bone-breaking misadventure, I survived. If you don't believe me about the force of these barrages, simply take a tour of the many cliff faces that have a perfectly shaped coyote silhouette etched into them. And the falls! Heaven help me! From heights unimaginable, I fell. Sometimes straight as an arrow, sometimes bouncing off canyon walls, sometimes alone, sometimes with cartoonishly large boulders that steadfastly refused to observe Newton's law of universal gravitation. I swear whether we fell at the same time or I fell seconds after, I always ended up underneath one as I hit the ground. And don't get me started on anvils!

One day, as I picked a boulder shard out of my soft palate and applied salve to my chapped lips (yes, coyotes have lips ... again, may I point you towards the Discovery Channel), it occurred to me that only the Devil could change the laws of nature. Of course! Using simple deductive logic, I made an incredible discovery. If we suppose that (a) destruction and torment in opposition to the laws of nature are the Devil's work, and (b) the Bird wreaks destruction and torment in opposition to the laws of nature, then can we not deduce that (c) the Bird is doing the Devil's work? The real question seemed to be, Was the Bird the Devil or just His representative in the arid wasteland of the American Southwest? *And*, if the Bird had the awesome power of the Devil, why was He keeping me alive? To torment me? To maim and injure but never destroy? I truly believed He was.

As I am sure you have ascertained, I am no idiot. I know when I've met my match. I did not believe I could defeat the Devil, so I changed tactics. (One doesn't evolve without adapting.) From that moment on, I tried to look upon Him as nothing more than a wasp. If I didn't bother Him, He wouldn't bother me. I admitted defeat and moved on. For two glorious weeks I moved on. And it was easy to do because of my Soulmate. You see, I had fallen in love.

The day after I had sworn never to chase that #%@#* Bird ever again, I saw her from atop my perch on a large granite outcropping by Fudd's Reach. She had a pelt of deep reddish-brown that shone in the harsh desert sun. Long black-tipped guard hairs formed a dark cross between her shoulders. My God, she was a beautiful bitch. (I am speaking of course scientifically, so no sniggering!) And she was interested in me. I can't tell you how refreshing it was to have someone admire me for my body and not my mind.

I don't know why the gods smiled upon me but I was happy for it. I had found the mate I wanted to spend the rest of my life with. The Bird was banished to the back of my brain, though every once in a while I started at the sound of a faint "meep meep" in the distance. Still, for two glorious weeks, I was like the others of my kind, hunting with a partner, sharing our prey, mating with primitive desire. Then, at the height of my happiness, the obsession returned. Slowly at first but quickly snowballing, as enticing to me as alcohol to the alcoholic. I started sneaking off, hatching plans, failing over and over in my quest, yet never surrendering to defeat. I made up excuses for my many absences. Things like "Heard about a new den that might be nice for us," or "I'm giving grooming lessons to help prevent sarcoptic mange in our friends," or, and I believe this was my low point, "Have to pee, just going to mark some territory." I thought I could hide my frequent forays into the desert, but no. My Soulmate tired of my distraction and she tried to lure me back with her ample feminine charms. It worked for a while, but it never took.

I suppose it was inevitable. One day I returned to our den, my pelt still smoking from an Electric Superhero Uniform misfire, to find our home empty and my Soulmate flown; not her alone but also the litter that she carried within her. My progeny. As I stood there, numb, the smell of my burnt fur filling my nostrils, God appeared to me. He appeared in the form of an enormous saguaro cactus (I knew it was him, I recognized the voice), and he told me that my greatest fear was correct. The Bird *was* the Devil, and I alone could destroy Him.

For the next few days, God appeared to me almost hourly, demanding that I kill the Devil. He didn't always appear as a cactus. Once he appeared as my Wolfman Jack poster; another time, a can of talcum powder. In all of those manifestations, though, he left out the important part. How should I kill the Devil? He said he would give me a sign. And he did.

The very next day, as I settled down to peruse the newest Company catalogue, a strange sudden wind tore it from my paws, sending it skidding in the dust. It came to rest face up and open to the page God wanted me to see.

God bless The Company! Their newest device made my heart soar. The Artificial Good Luck Generator! Brilliant—and perfect for me. I can admit, in hindsight, that while some of my misadventures were due to my negligence or hastiness—whatever—most were due to plain old bad luck. This time there would be no mistakes. Good luck was guaranteed! I placed my order (I got a bonus gift!) and waited for delivery. The Company has the most advanced delivery system known to man or coyote. Twenty-seven minutes after placing the order, I had my package.

I opened the box and stood in awe of the incredible contraption in front of me. I read the instructions and reread them. I made sure I missed nothing in the fine print and memorized each step. It was fairly simple, but from experience I knew I could not be cocky.

The day of reckoning dawned. I felt the desert wind blowing in my face. That was a good sign: the Devil always ran with the wind behind Him. In the distance I heard the "meep meep" that never failed to make my back arch and my teeth grind. I could see the dust cloud as He made His way towards me. I activated the Good Luck Generator and closed my mind to everything except the whispering of God. I think I giggled. Closer and closer He came.

"He's coming," God whispered in my ear.

I was, for the first time in my cursed life, completely calm. My heart rate slowed, my senses became acute. I could smell a mosquito 500 yards to my left; he'd had a burrito for lunch. I could hear a rabbit burrowing in the ground almost half a kilometre behind me, and if I wasn't mistaken, there was a duck with him. He was right, he should have turned left at Albuquerque. I could feel the wind, soft and warm, rippling through my fur. And I could see Him—the Devil—with almost alarming clarity. I wondered what was going through His mind at that moment. Did He anticipate some hellish fun at the hapless coyote's expense?

Then it happened.

Twenty yards from where I stood, the Devil did something He had never done before.

He tripped.

At breakneck speed that stupid Bird tripped! I watched as He tumbled and somersaulted and ended up splayed on the ground at my feet. He looked up at me through those long, dusty lashes with pain and fear in His eyes. Delicious fear. I bent down to Him, slowly, drinking it all in. And as I looked at His torn feathers and broken, bloody beak, I was reminded of how He had destroyed *my* life. From the countless humiliations of falling through canyons, getting crushed by anvils, and run over by trains, I had watched Him make a mockery of the laws of nature and science. He had made me destroy my love, my chance at a family.

I sank my teeth into His soft neck, ignoring the terrified

"meep meep" He gurgled with His last breath. Warm blood splashed onto my face and flowed down my throat as I shook Him violently, breaking His neck. His eyes clouded and His body went limp, but nothing, certainly not pity, would ease my blood lust. I devoured Him, feathers, beak, bones, and all. I laughed into His dead eyes as I pulled His drumsticks apart.

Then, as quickly as it had come, the rage left me. I was lying on the ground, covered in Bird viscera with a feather stuck to my cheek with blood. My chest heaved with the pounding of my heart. I had done it! I had killed the Devil. Nothing more to haunt me! Nothing more to fill my days and nights! Nothing more ... at all.

That was where they found me two days later, still crying.

I have no idea where they took me. I surmise it isn't your usual animal detention centre. I have been studied, probed, injected, and cut. But I think I scared them. I overheard two of the orderlies say, "The freak gets it tonight." What, no chance to defend myself? No trial? No matter. I wonder if they can actually kill me. Lethal injection? Ha! They'll have to do better than that.

I'm looking out my cell window as I write this. The moon is up. I'm looking at my Soulmate, standing quite a distance away, waiting for me. I howled every hour from the moment I was put in here, hoping she would hear, and she did. She came back for me.

My makeshift device, fashioned from bedsprings and a defunct transistor, has neatly blown the bars from my window and I'm free to escape. (Admit it. You are impressed that I am writing a memoir, conducting a jailbreak, and courting my woman all at the same time. Admit it.)

And now the hardest part ... or is it the easiest? Remember my bonus gift? The little freebie that The Company tossed in with the Artificial Good Luck Generator? I laughed when I saw it. PERMANENT DE-EVOLVER PILLS. The pills, through a complex chemical process, permeate cell membranes to ... Look, I'll make it simple. I take the pill, I de-evolve into an average coyote. No talking, no inventing, no super-genius. Just a coyote. Sounds good to me. I never really fit into the human world anyway. The pants chafed.

I take the pill. I feel calm. This is the right choice for me, for her, for the litter. All I want is them. With my family, perhaps I can get the peace I've never had on my own. This is how I shall leave. Do not pity me. My mind is far, far clearer than I ever thought possible. I am far, far happier than I have ever hoped.

It is a far, far, better thing that I do, than I have ever done; it is a far, far better rest that I go to than I have ever known.

The Cat
and My Dad

INSPIRED BY DR. SEUSS'S
THE CAT IN THE HAT

The sun never showed.
It rained and it poured.
So dreary and depressing
That I stayed indoors.

> Though to tell you the truth,
> Even if it were sunny,
> We wouldn't *dare* step outside,
> Not for all the world's money.

Not out in the front yard,
Or even the back.
No fresh air for us
Since the zombies attacked!

> Had it been just a month
> Since the world fell apart?
> How did it begin?
> When did it all start?

Ah, yes, I remember,
It comes now in flashes.
It started with people
Getting itchy red rashes.

There was coughing and hacking
And barfing and sores
That smelled truly awful—
Ghastly symptoms GALORE!

Then a flux and a fever
An ache in the head,
Then zippo and presto—
All the victims dropped dead.

But they didn't stay that way—
Proper corpses just rot.
These acted up
The whole naughty lot.

They groaned and they crawled,
They staggered and jerked,
Out of cars, schools, and malls
And the places they worked.

The world was in turmoil,
No one was elated,
Except those who quite wisely
Had loved ones cremated.

No one knows why—
Science offers no reason
Why the zombies attacked
In this precise season.

Why, no matter your pay scale,
Your class, or your height,
You might rise up a zombie
With a brain appetite.

There were bride and groom zombies
Recently wed,
A Ralph Lauren zombie—
Haute couture for the dead.

There were zombies of Science,
Of Arts, and of Maths.
Some that had showers
While others took baths.

Life wasn't good,
In fact life was bad.
My major worry?
What happened to Dad?

He had gone off to work
Like he did every day.
Jumped in his car
(The blue Chevrolet).

I waved from the window,
As I usually did,
In my jammies while petting
Our cat, Mr. Sid.

Dad smiled and waved
In his nice dadly way.
But we haven't seen him
Since that pre-zombie day.

Was he eaten by zombies?
Did he die, then come back?
Was he Frank-en-stein-stag-ger-ing
Hunting a snack?

I hope that he's living,
That he's safe and okay.
We need him back home
And we need him today!

'Cause my mom's catatonic,
She's developed bulimia.
'Cause Mr. Sid's dying
From feline leukemia.

I think it's the stress
From the zombie attack
Making everyone's health
Go so far off track.

As man of the house
I'll keep family together,
But being just eight
Now's the end of my tether.

I'm feeling quite weary,
Looking out at the rain,
At zombies a-wandering
Moaning (hungrily), "Braaaiiinnns."

I have to admit
It's annoying to hear.
I mean, mix it up sometimes—
How 'bout asking for beer?

Then again, a drunk zombie
Wouldn't be very good.
(Though it'd move slower yet
Than a sober one could.)

As I thought about Dad,
I spied up the road
A blue Chevrolet gunning
Towards our abode!

At the sound Mom jumped up
With hope in her smile.
Mr. Sid promptly barfed
On the clean kitchen tile.

I watched as the car
Drew nearer and nearer.
I watched as the face
Of the driver grew clearer.

The Chevy turned into
Our driveway and parked.
The door slowly opened,
The neighbour's dog barked.

Out crept my dad,
Limb by limb like a spider,
With eyes open wide
And his mouth open wider.

He'd turned into a zombie
Neither dead nor alive!
And he'd come home to eat us!
(Dinner's always at five.)

He loped and he shambled,
He deadwalked and swayed.
Till he'd mounted the steps
Of the veranda he'd made.

We looked on with horror
When he tried the doorknob.
While he twisted and yanked it
Mom stifled a sob.

Then my poor zombie father
Remembered his keys,
Dropped them, then caught them
Between his dead knees.

As he ran into trouble
Fitting key into lock,
My dad started swearing—
It came as a shock!

My dad never swore
Not even a "damn it!"
Now he cursed like a sailor
In a drama by Mamet.

But then he calmed down,
Counted one, two, three, four,
An audible click—
He'd unlocked our front door.

That spurred us to action—
We leapt to our feet.
Mom grabbed me and the cat
And beat a hasty retreat!

She ran for the door
That led to downstairs.
"Follow me!" she ordered,
"And don't you be scared!"

Don't be scared? Are you joking?
I threw Mom a glance.
I was seconds away
From peeing my pants!

> We flew down the stairwell—
> No braking or break—
> But that's when it struck me:
> Classic rookie mistake.

Trapped in the basement—
Oh, what were we thinking?
There's nowhere to go!
It started to sink in ...

> With no place to run,
> And nowhere to hide,
> We were totally done for.
> I started to cry.

Dad came down the stairs,
Looking clearly deranged.
Since the last time I'd seen him
He'd totally changed.

> His hair, neatly parted,
> Was now dappled with mud.
> His teeth, once so gleaming,
> Were now stained with blood.

His eyes had a glint,
His intent was quite plain.
He spoke but one word.
You guessed it: "Brraaiinn."

But amazingly then—
Oh, brave Mr. Sid!
He did what no feline
Could *ever* have did.

He jumped at my father
With claws and teeth gnashing;
My father fell gagging—
From Sid's breath or the slashing?

Now was my chance!
Find a weapon to use!
I saw scissors, a golf club,
A pair of spiked shoes.

I needed a crossbow,
A machete, a gun.
But being Canadians,
Alas, we had none.

My father rose up,
So ferocious but dumb,
And he shambled and lurched
Towards Mr. Sid and my mom.

It was then that I spied them
Above the Goodyears,
Hanging up on a hook—
Sharpened gardening shears!

    I ran to the cutters,
    Grabbed them right off the wall.
    Then turned to my father
    Fiercely dreading it all.

Mom shouted, "Kill him!
Kill your father right now!"
Though I heard her I paused—
Could I do it? And how?

    Zombie Dad doddered closer,
    He walked as though lame.
    He looked at me strangely,
    Then croaked out my name.

He remembered my name!
My heart swelled with pride.
Since he'd uttered my name,
Was my real dad inside?

    As if to give answer,
    He smiled a big smile,
    It stretched for so long
    That up rose my bile.

His teeth seemed to sharpen.
His eyes narrowed black.
He looked at me, drooling ...
His cranial snack.

I heard my mom screaming,
"Now! Kill him now, son!
Stab him and kill him
Don't stop till it's done."

I stood there not moving;
Just feeling real bad.
But I think that that's normal,
Before killing your dad.

I took a deep breath,
Faked a step to my left,
Spun right and then stuck
The shears right through his neck.

He howled and he screamed
As he fell to the ground,
He gulped and he sputtered
Then thrashed all around.

When it finally ended,
And Zombie Dad died,
He lay by my bike,
With his head at his side.

We were safe in our basement
In the workshop Dad built.
I'd saved our three lives,
But was tortured with guilt.

Mom was still crying,
You'd expect that she would.
She kissed me and hugged me,
Said, "Son, you did good."

But should I have killed him?
Dispatched him like that?
Well what would YOU do?
If a zombie attacked?

Franken's Time

INSPIRED BY MARY SHELLEY'S
FRANKENSTEIN

I am by birth a Genevese, and my family is one of the most distinguished of that republic. Our name is spoken with reverence in every corner of our country, with a tone usually reserved for royalty or clergy. For as long as the mighty Rhone has fed the crystalline waters of Lake Geneva on its way to France (like a drunken tourist in search of Gallic grapes), our family has supplied Switzerland with chickens for its roasting pans, eggs for its larders, and feathers for its pallets. Whether prosperous or beggarly, the Swiss have enjoyed the fruits of my family's labour for hundreds of years.

The grandest poultry farm in Europe—nay, the world—sits upon five acres of verdant alpine meadow, bordered on three sides by immense forests of beech and oak, and on the fourth by a majestic cliff that overlooks Lake Geneva. It is a glorious place. Edelweiss, gentians, and buttercups dot the meadow in the spring and summer. In the fall, russet and amber leaves fall to the forest floor, while through the winter months, snow drapes the gingerbread eaves of my Swiss chalet in softest folds of white.

A stone's throw from the chalet, nestled against a copse of beech, is the Great Barn, rough timbered and sturdy.

Step through the open doors and hear a cacophony of industry—clucking, rustling, fluttering industry. In the slanting sunlight, sparkling with dust motes, sit the finest Appenzellers and Schweizers in the world. Row upon row, handsome blue-legged specimens with well-spread tails, full hackles, and tight, glossy black plumage roost in splendour.

The rearing of chickens is a noble, time-honoured tradition, but one that comes with its share of misconceptions. The general populace thinks of chickens as the great dullards (not to mention the great cowards) of all of God's creatures. Who among us has not harshly judged the species after watching a sturdy specimen peck the eyes from a weakened brother? Scatter and cluck at the first sign of trouble? Defecate on its feet, and then trample its offspring? (A German gentleman in town did the very same, but it was agreed he was a very troubled soul.)

Who among us has not thought, "A chicken's only purpose is to provide meat and eggs"? And in general, I must agree, for my livelihood depends upon it. A chicken's life has little meaning outside the farm wife's skillet, and yet—and yet it is not always so. It is not always the way of poultry to sit idly in the coop, or peck for grubs in the dirt. It certainly was not the case of an amazing Schweizer named Franken, whose great lust for life changed the course of my own.

Now, as a rule, I do not name my chickens. It's harder to grip the axe when the head you're chopping off belongs to Liesl, Brigitta, or Marta. Slaughtering the nameless is infinitely easier, as any politician will attest. But my customary resolve weakened the moment I laid eyes on a fluffy Schweizer chick, hatched in the spring of 1918, on a beautiful cloudless day that set the milkmaid to yodelling. From the very start, there was something about this sweet chick that set it apart from the rest of its kind. An attentiveness of his surroundings, an appreciation of the momentousness of his hatching, an awareness of the sanctity of his own life.

I loved him at once.

His enthusiastic curiosity immediately endeared him to me. Just days after emerging from the egg, he ran wildly around the property, his little chicken legs pumping, drinking in every tree, flower, and stone. He studied a small piece of quartz with the intensity of a geologist, turning it over with his tiny claws so that he could explore every facet. He splashed around in a small puddle with the joy of a young child. While I dried him off, he fell asleep in my palm. Soon, whenever I came within his sightline, he greeted me with a small hop that never failed to make me smile. And for some reason, this newborn Schweizer chick reminded me of my second cousin, Franken. Maybe it was the soft brown of his eyes, or the tilt of his head when I spoke to him. Perhaps it was because they both loved drinking from a water dish. It doesn't really matter what the reason—the little chicken's innate lovability reminded me of my cherished relative. And so I named him Franken.

In the weeks following his hatching, Franken quickly became my favourite. In all my years in this profession, I had never showed affection for one bird over another. In fact, I don't think I had ever shown affection at all. But Franken changed that. He was devoted to me. He followed me as I undertook the day's routine. As I filled the feeder with my secret mix and poured fresh water into the drinker, Franken herded the others so that they did not get in my way, or I in theirs. As I collected eggs from the coop each morning, Franken stood before the roosts and cooed softly to the hens, calming their nerves and allowing me to go about my business without disturbing them. When I hung my clothes to dry on the drying line, Franken hopped upon a picnic table and offered up clothes pegs in his beak. The others in the flock looked to him almost immediately as their leader, so great was his natural inborn ability.

Perhaps if I had a wife and family, I would not have grown so attached to this peculiar little fowl that burrowed his way into my heart. Unfortunately, I tended towards the life of a hermit, so I rarely came in contact with a living soul, let alone someone I could share a life with. That is, until I spied a beautiful young woman named Gretl, whilst on one of my infrequent forays into the town. Although we had spoken but a few polite words to each other, my deep awkwardness and damnable shyness kept me from pursuing something that could have bloomed into romance. But in this, too, Franken would have a hand to play.

As the weeks turned into months, Franken matured into a handsome cockerel and we got into the practice of taking long walks around the property once our daily chores were complete. We took different routes through the many trails and paths that coursed through the forests around the farm. It was during one of these pleasant forays that I suddenly found myself talking to my feathered charge about the lovely Gretl.

"I do not think I shall every fully comprehend the fairer sex, Franken."

Franken turned to me, listening intently as he hopped along.

"There is a lass in town. Her name is Gretl. You've not met her."

"Puk-puk," he clucked encouragingly.

"For a reason not clear to me, whenever I am close to her, my words desert me like rats from a sinking ship."

Franken stopped and looked at me. He raised his chicken wings. "Puck-puck?"

"No, it is not the same at all. There are myriad differences between the male and the female."

"Puk-Puke!"

I blushed. "No, I mean other things. But maybe you're right, and we are not so different after all."

Franken clucked knowingly and scratched modestly in the dirt.

We talked—or rather, *I* talked and Franken listened raptly—for an hour. At the end of it, I felt unburdened and quite clear on what I should do next regarding the fair Gretl. Franken was my trusted confidant, and together, over the following days, we spent hours going over the parts of my life that until that point had remained unspoken and unexplored.

It was during one of these conversations that the most peculiar thing happened. We were in my library taking tea. ("Library" might be a grandiose description, as it was merely a room with one bookcase. But although it was paltry in comparison to the great libraries of Europe, I was proud of my collection's eclectic nature. Classic novels alongside manuals and textbooks on biology and engineering were my standard reading material.) Seated in my reading chair, I was talking of some inconsequential thing or another when I realized that Franken wasn't listening to me. He was standing on my desk peering at an open copy of *Jude the Obscure*. I laughed, for it was a sight that tickled me. I stopped laughing when I noticed that he was tracing his scaly talon down the margin and then using his beak to turn the page. He was not merely looking at the book. He was reading it! I am sure I sound quite mad, and for a moment I myself feared that I had leapt full bore over the line that separates the rational from the insane. Had I been spending too much time alone?

"Franken!" I exclaimed. "What are you doing?"

Franken turned to me and widened his eyes as if to say, "What does it look like?" (Franken did not suffer fools gladly. Millie, my Bouvier Suisse, still had the scratches on her snout to prove it.)

To ease my mind, I decided to test him on his comprehension. "Franken, what is the name of Jude's first wife? Cluck once for Annabella, twice for Cinderella, and three times for Arabella."

Franken clucked three times.

Filled with a growing excitement, I questioned him with more multiple choices. Questions about the themes of fixed class boundaries, criticisms of marriage, and Christianity. To my astonishment and great pride, he answered each one correctly.

Have you ever had someone attempt to explain to you the love they have for their child? How it differs from every other form of love? It is absolutely impossible to convey without experiencing it. That night with Franken, I finally understood. I was filled with pride for what he could do, and my affection for him was so intense I felt I would burst. That night Franken transformed from darling pet to boon companion. He became my closest friend, my family.

In the following weeks we fell into an even more peaceful and companionable routine. Our days were spent immersed in the duties of chicken farming with frequent philosophical debates on the nature of love and companionship. (My feelings for Gretl had deepened and I needed an outlet.) Our nights were spent reading, I by the fire with a glass of port, Franken on the desk with a small bowl of seed.

After *Jude the Obscure*, Franken moved on to *Tess of the D'Urbervilles*, followed by the Russian masters: Tolstoy and Dostoyevsky. It worried me that his taste in novels ran to the bleak, but Franken refused to read lighter fare. I had placed both *Don Quixote* and *The Life and Opinions of Tristram Shandy, Gentleman* on his desk, two of the most exceedingly humorous books in my somewhat limited collection, but after perusing a few pages of each, he stuck his beak in the air and glared at me balefully before plucking the Brontës from my shelf. The depressive sisters then led to *Oliver Twist, The Old Curiosity Shop*, and Émile Zola's *Germinal*. Franken's thirst for literature was unquenchable. Every once in a while he would dip into old biology, physics, or chemistry textbooks, but they never held his attention for long; he always returned to the classics.

It was shortly after Franken had finished Hans Christian Andersen's *The Little Match Girl* that we planned a rare trip into town. It was market day, my favourite time of the month. The streets were bustling with vendors selling everything from books to bolts of cloth to livestock. Franken was quickly exhausting the resources of my modest library, so I thought I would stock up on some new reading material for him, and at the same time, perhaps, increase my flock with a few canny purchases. Franken perched upon my shoulder so we would not become separated in the crowds, which I fear made me look like a dull and impecunious pirate. But it never occurred to me to leave Franken at home on the farm, so close had we become that spring. As we made our way along the cobblestoned streets of the village that dated from medieval times, I spied Gretl looking over a booth filled with silk scarves.

"That is the woman I was telling you about," I whispered out of the corner of my mouth. Franken gave an approving cluck and squeezed my shoulder. And so he should have. Gretl's beauty would have caused an artist misery, for no one on Earth had the skill to capture the perfection of her face. Her hair was a coppery red that blazed in the sun. Her eyes were bluer than the ocean and combined a dazzling innocence with a knowing mischievousness. Propriety stops me from describing the rest of her form, but rest assured, Gentle Reader, everything was exactly as it should be.

"Should I go over, Franken? No, she probably ..."

Franken pecked mercilessly at my ear.

"Ow! What are you doing?"

Franken tilted his head towards Gretl and prodded me to go to her.

"No, Franken, I don't think I should. Ow!" Another peck came, followed by another. "All right! All right!"

Franken eyed me and cocked his comb.

I made my way over to the brightly coloured stall until I stood slightly behind Gretl. She was still intent on the silken scarves and had not noticed my approach.

"I think that green one would look quite lovely on you."

She turned to me and smiled. "Oh, Mr. Gosteli. How lovely to see you. Do you think so?" Her eyes flitted to Franken perched upon my shoulder, and her brows raised in question.

"Oh, this is my Schweizer. Uh ... One of my chickens. Uh ... A very special Schweizer cockerel."

Franken jumped gingerly from my shoulder onto Gretl's. He nuzzled her cheek affectionately and clucked. I have never been envious of a chicken in my life, but at that moment I wished to trade places with my friend. Gretl for her part seemed delighted with Franken's pluck. Not many women would be so calm and composed when leapt upon by a fowl, but Gretl was grace personified.

"Oh, how perfectly charming!" Gretl stroked Franken's beak gently and laughed in delight. "How very sweet! What is his name?"

"Franken," I said, her musical laugh still echoing in my ears.

"Well, Franken, I hope we shall get to know each other better."

"Puk-puk," he agreed, and ducked his head shyly.

Franken was charming her! I took his cue. "There is a small restaurant around the corner, with the most charming terrace. If indeed you would like to get to know him better, may I suggest a pastis?"

Her eyes locked on mine and she smiled her heart-stopping smile. "That sounds lovely."

I took her arm and escorted her around the corner. To this day I have no idea what we talked about, so enchanted was I, but we whiled away two hours on the terrace, beneath a trellis of bougainvillea. That was just as well, since the proprietor had some misgivings about Franken being inside the establishment. We were so besotted with each other that it wasn't until we were leaving that I noticed Franken wasn't with us.

"Did you see where he went?" I asked Gretl, trying to keep the panic out of my voice.

"No, I didn't. But he couldn't have gotten far. I'll help you find him."

We searched the streets, the vendors, the doorways and alleys. I was about to give up hope when I heard a familiar cluck. I turned and there he was, running in circles at a stall that sold chickens.

"Franken!" I shouted, drowning in relief. "Bad boy! What are you doing?"

Gretl whispered in my ear, her closeness drawing the blood from my head, almost making me swoon: "I believe that the 'bad boy' is doing what bad boys have been doing since time began."

Franken was standing in front of a beautiful caged Appenzeller pullet, and was obviously smitten. Appenzellers, though respectable egg producers, are largely raised as show chickens, and I was not in need of another. I raised my eyebrow skeptically.

"Perhaps you should purchase her for your friend," Gretl urged.

"Hmm. I don't really need an Appenzeller. She is a different breed from Franken."

"I don't think that matters when it comes to love, do you?"

"Well. That is ..." I trailed off, lost in her eyes.

"Mr. Gosteli, I thought you were a romantic. I cannot believe that you would be an obstacle to true love."

"No. Certainly not. I wouldn't ..."

"I mean, how monstrous it would be if Franken was denied what all creatures desire. Monstrous, indeed." There was a teasing quality in her voice.

"Excuse me for a moment, will you? I have to see a man about a chicken."

I called her Evelyn, for no other reason than that Franken crowed when I suggested the name. She and Franken spent considerable time together in those first few days, and I worried that Franken preferred her company to mine. If I hadn't been in the midst of courting Gretl, I am sure I would have been jealous. Of course Franken would want to spend time with someone of his own species, if not genus, though I often wondered to myself what they could possibly have in common.

Evelyn took no notice of the classics, except once when she pecked a bit of the corner of *Romeo and Juliet*. That did seem to irk Franken; his hackles raised in annoyance, but he quickly recovered himself and nudged her towards his bowl of seed on the desk. The incident caused no lasting acrimony. It was then that I realized that chickens are no different from humans in many ways. Beauty is often valued above intellectual acuity.

Franken and I introduced our two ladies to many of our

daily rituals, and the four of us spent many lovely times walking through the woods, sharing laughs and clucks. It seemed the world was our oyster and all was right in our little love haven.

But then misfortune visited our idyllic farm.

I was repairing a leak in the drinker in the Great Barn when Franken came running, his wattles flapping. I could see by the crazed look in his eyes that something was terribly wrong. I followed him back to Evelyn's roost, to find her looking a little pale and drawn. I checked her wings and her feet for wounds, and finding none, chastised Franken for the false alarm.

To his credit, Franken didn't leave Evelyn's side, but perched upon the window sill nearby where he could keep an eye on her.

I didn't see it at first, but it all became clearer in the next few days. It started with Evelyn's loss of appetite, and soon she had no appetite at all. Franken implored her to eat some seed, even plucking some up in his beak and tossing it at her feet. But she ate nothing. Shortly after that a great amount of blood appeared in the droppings at the bottom of her nest.

Gretl grew as concerned about the quick deterioration of Evelyn's health as Franken, and spent much time in the Great Barn encouraging her to eat. I was concerned too, but from my experience raising chickens, I knew that nothing could be done.

Evelyn had coccidiosis, a miserable parasite that attacked her small intestine. No doubt she was infected when I brought her home that first day. None of my other hens had become ill, so I quarantined her in an attempt to prevent an outbreak. Alas, I had diagnosed Evelyn too late to help her in any way. It was only a matter of time, but I had not the heart to tell Franken or Gretl.

Gretl arrived at the farm early one morning with a little basket under her arm containing chicken broth. Franken crowed with untempered horror at the sight, flapping his wings and running in circles. I quietly explained to Gretl the inappropriateness of her well-intended gesture, and she burst into tears at her thoughtlessness. "Cannibalism!" she whispered in horror. Never had I felt so helpless. Evelyn died the next day.

Franken was inconsolable. His comb visibly drooped and his eyes were listless. Gretl cradled him in her lap and stroked his wings, but I think Franken was beyond comforting. We had a funeral for Evelyn and buried her underneath a young beech tree on the property, marked with a lovely cross that Gretl had made herself. After I spoke a few words, Franken let out a blood-curdling crow filled with despair and anguish. He perched on a low-hanging bough of the beech and refused to leave her grave for two days.

As time passed, Franken drifted through his days. Even our evening ritual seemed to bring him no joy. One night I noticed him reading a pamphlet on the raising of poultry that I had neglected to tuck inside the desk drawer. Halfway through it, he looked up at me with sorrow. It didn't dawn on me at the time, but now I comprehend fully what that glance meant. That was the moment Franken realized that he was ... livestock. A commodity, a tool of the trade, not even possessing the stature of the family pet. I believe that up until that moment, Franken believed that he was just a shorter feathery version of a human being. His eyes filled with tears, and he set his beak in a grim line. I could offer him no comfort. That night I fell into a fitful and uneasy sleep.

Over the next few weeks, Franken rallied to become a somewhat subdued version of himself. He joined Gretl and me on our walks past Evelyn's grave. He started reading again, and I took that as a good sign. And as ever, his choice of material was ambitious, if unusual. The Bible had recently become the tome he most often buried his beak in. I glanced at the passage the Good Book was opened to: John 11:25–26.

"Jesus said unto her, I am the resurrection, and the life: he that believeth in me, though he were dead, yet shall he live: and whosoever liveth and believeth in me shall never die."

Right beside it lay Galvani's text on galvanism: *De viribus electricitatis in motu musculari.* Perhaps I should have paid more attention. I wish now that I had.

Three weeks after Evelyn's passing, Gretl paid me another visit. We sat on the veranda, with Franken pacing at the stairs, staring into space. We talked of many things and partook in a little gossip. Franken took no interest, until Gretl said, "I heard in town that a large storm is coming this way, probably two days from now. I must confess, rough weather scares me."

"Then why do you not come here and spend the day? From this vantage point you can see the storm come in over the lake. It really is quite beautiful in its way. Perhaps you could learn to quell your fear, and I would love to have your company."

She smiled shyly and we made a date. She would come in the afternoon for a picnic before the storm hit, then we would watch it together from the safety of the farmhouse. Franken stared at us with interested eyes and cocked his noble head.

Intent as I was on getting everything together for my stormy rendezvous, I failed to notice Franken's declining spirits. Nor did I observe the disappearance of particular objects from around the house and shed.

The day of our date dawned gentle and fair. In the late morning Gretl arrived, and we enjoyed a lovely, leisurely picnic on the hillside. We were enjoying each other's company immensely, and I had even been so bold as to steal a kiss, leaving us both quite breathless. But as we settled ourselves on the veranda to watch the storm roll in, I was suddenly grasped by a sense of foreboding.

"What is it, darling?" Gretl asked affectionately.

"Have you noticed Franken about?"

"No, now that you mention it. I haven't seen him all day."

I had secured the henhouse for the impending squall, and not seeing him there, supposed that my friend had retired to the house to wait out the storm. I was gripped with panic. We searched the house room by room, but Franken was nowhere to be found. The coming storm rattled the windows, and distant arcs of lightning brightened the dim interior of the library. A crack of thunder split the sky at the moment that my eye fell upon Franken's reading material: Galvani's text on reanimating dead cells.

A thought hit me with almost physical force. "Evelyn!"

We ran to the beech tree where Evelyn was buried. Wind whipped the leaves above us as we gazed at the horror at our feet. The gravesite had been recently disturbed and Evelyn's body was gone.

Just then, lightning struck the end of my property line where a small dirt road separated my home from the edge of the cliff that overlooked Lake Geneva. I squinted and could barely make out a structure that seemed to attract Nature's wrath. Lightning bolts zigzagged in the dark sky overhead. Below, Franken toiled at some mysterious purpose; his body was bent double against the wind. Three more times the lightning struck that unholy spot. Then I heard that blood-curdling crow—the very same one Franken had unleashed at Evelyn's burial.

"Franken!" I screamed, but my words were torn from my lips by the ferocity of the storm. I made my way across the meadow to the rough scaffolding near the edge of the cliff. My clothes were pinned against my body by wind and rain, and I tried to shield Gretl from the worst of it as she followed close behind me. We drew near, but Franken had already left that damnable spot. Fighting the wind, looking like an avian Heathcliff making his way across the moors, Franken was crossing the road.

There was nothing there except for the cliff. Despair gripped my heart as I recalled Franken's grief and depression, how he pored over the Bible in the day's following Evelyn's death. That's why Franken is crossing the road, I realized with horror! To get to the *Other Side*.

As we approached the rough-hewn scaffolding, the air was full of the scent of roasted chicken. It pains me to remember that I involuntarily salivated. As my eyes took in the terrible scene, I realized that Franken had somehow put together a makeshift laboratory. Evelyn had been placed between two large metal spikes, and her earthly remains bathed in some unknown solution. Franken had tried to reanimate her, but it had all gone horribly wrong. Charred feathers lay strewn about, and poor Evelyn's carcass was scorched and blackened. Franken, driven mad with grief, had tried to bring his love back from the dead, but had succeeded only in barbecuing her.

My only thoughts were of Franken. And as I ran with all my might to catch up with my dearest friend, I knew deep in my marrow that I had not the time nor the speed to stop what was happening. Gretl and I screamed at Franken to stop, to reconsider, to live. But he ignored our cries and increased his pace. He was never much of a runner (he could sprint for a very limited time), but Franken was an excellent fast walker. Adrenalin pushed me to the limit, so that I was able to close the gap between us to approximately fifty yards. But it was still too far. I kept running, tears stinging my eyes, wind whipping my hair, but to no avail.

Franken paused at the edge of the precipice, the wind tearing through his feathers. Just before he jumped, he turned to me and smiled. It took quite an effort to contort his beak, but Franken smiled: a sad, sweet, broken-hearted smile.

I ran to the spot where my friend had stood mere seconds before. Below me, ceaseless waves crashed upon the shore, and above me, the heavens continued to rage ...

Franken's small, sturdy body floated on the churning waters of Lake Geneva, a small speck. I prayed that he was at peace. Tears, mixed with the driving rain, poured down my face as I stood at the edge of the cliff watching his body float away. Gretl reached me and put a tender arm around my shoulders. Together we wept.

We stood watching as he floated farther and farther from shore. **He was soon borne away by the waves and lost in darkness and distance.**

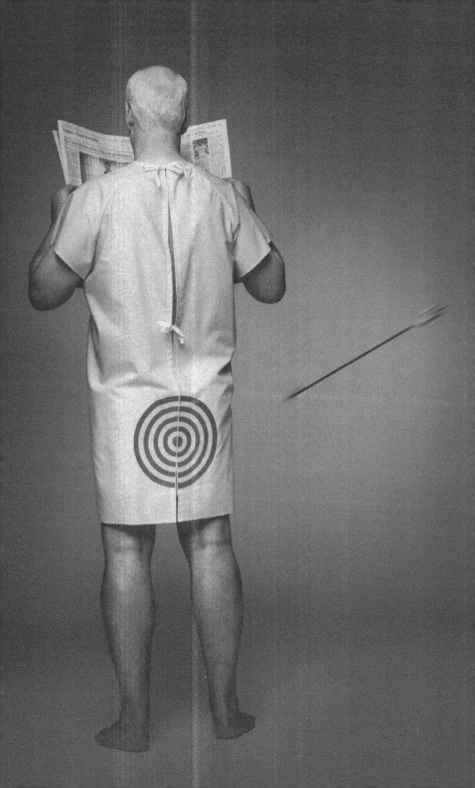

Waterhouse Five

INSPIRED BY KURT VONNEGUT'S
SLAUGHTERHOUSE-FIVE

All this happened, more or less. Don't focus on the less. The less is unimportant. A few bits of dialogue here and there may be slightly changed or exaggerated. Never a big deal, unless you're arguing with your spouse. The more of the "more or less" is the main thing. These events did actually happen. There is documented evidence proving it. Trust me, I'm the narrator. And narrators never lie.

Billy Jonah was the unluckiest man in history. Unluckier than Tsutomu Yamaguchi, who was having breakfast in Hiroshima at 8:15 A.M. on August 6, 1945, when the A-bomb detonated and destroyed his apartment building. Tsutomu survived, but three days later he travelled to Nagasaki to convalesce. Unluckier than Terry Rydell, who was hit by lightning seven times. On the seventh and final time, he was struck while flying a kite beside the train tracks of his Kingston-area home. His body was completely magnetized, which, unfortunately, resulted in a three-hour ride courtesy of a Via train en route to Montreal. The worst part wasn't the mode of travel—it was the destination. Terry hated bagels and jazz. And the Habs.

Now to be sure, Billy didn't have the dramatic, traumatic, life-threatening bad luck that Tsutomu and

Terry did. That one big misadventure that would put him in the "Odd but True" section of the newspaper seemed to elude him. Sometimes he wished it would happen in one big chunk. But his bad luck was more like a constant stream of unfortunateness; an irritating and incessant dribble of misfortune.

Minor things went wrong in Billy's personal life and professional life every day. One Monday morning, as Billy walked to work, a disoriented bat flew into his head with such force that it almost knocked him over. As he grabbed on to a lamppost for support, a German shepherd escaped his leash, bounded over to him, and humped his leg like a sailor on VE day. Then there was the time, only three seconds before giving a speech at his younger brother's wedding, that an inebriated waiter spilled a gallon of jalapeño blue cheese dressing straight onto Billy's crotch. Billy *hated* public speaking. The tenants of the apartment building that Billy lived in three years ago are still talking about the day when a mysterious gust of wind slammed his door closed as he was picking up the morning newspaper, pushing him into the middle of the hallway naked as a newborn babe.

And yet, a lovelier, more positive man you could never hope to meet. Billy Jonah lived life with a constant smile on his lips; he happily held doors for women and children, he never failed to nod or say hello to anyone who passed him in the street, and he paused to smell every flower, no matter if the bee drinking its nectar got lodged in his nostril, requiring an emergency room visit and a shot of epinephrine to the heart. It seemed cruel that someone so pure of spirit and intent should be repeatedly kicked in the balls by life. Yes, Billy had little victories, like getting the last sticky bun at the local bakery, or winning a free ticket in the lottery. They raised his hopes that they might mark the turning point in his fortunes. But alas and alack, it never seemed to be.

On the day that Billy Jonah became a legend in the annals of misfortune, he was trying to find a way to make Cramer's Cheese Chunks sound appetizing. He was failing spectacularly. Writing copy for an ad agency was a pretty entertaining gig—most of the time. But Billy had made the cardinal mistake on this particular campaign. He'd actually *tasted* a Cramer's Cheese Chunk. Billy didn't have a problem with the Cramer part: the product was indeed made by the Cramer Dairy Company. And, as one could plainly see, it did come in chunks. The cheese part was the part that flummoxed him. No cheese produced anywhere in the world tasted like this bright orange, sweaty-foot-smelling dollop of fake food. Still, it was a sight better than how he felt the rest of his afternoon was going to go.

Billy had a doctor's appointment. Billy was leery of doctors. Of course, given his life experience, that wasn't totally illogical. When bad luck is your constant companion, going to a man in a white coat whose job it is to discover how your body is betraying you is not something you look forward to. Still, Billy tried, as he always did, to find the positive in every situation. He had recently turned fifty and it had been a while since he had had an annual. A clean bill of health always provided a sense of calm, Billy reasoned, and a sense of calm was always welcome in his world. True, the examination could reveal a disorder of some sort, perhaps a tumour—but these things would still be there if Billy didn't go to a doctor, and wasn't it better to nip these things in the bud?

So, after eight hours of working in a small grey cubicle coming up with a commercial spot for Cramer's Cheese Chunks, he shut down his computer, spilled coffee over his campaign notes, cut his thumb on a piece of foolscap, and readied himself for Dr. Feldman's.

Making his way out onto the street, Billy noticed that Tommy One-Bird was working the corner. One-Bird was the only person who made Billy feel lucky. A small, wizened, full-blooded Navajo, One-Bird begged and hustled money from passersby. He wore old army fatigues with his name stitched over his breast pocket. No one knew what One-Bird's history was, but he was extremely odd. Billy wondered if he'd suffered a grave misfortune of his own, like a traumatic brain injury. For when One-Bird spoke, it was total gibberish. Billy had, at first, assumed that One-Bird was speaking in his native tongue, but as he grew accustomed to Tommy One-Bird's curious way of speaking, Billy could pick out English words. Strangest of all was that the little Navajo spoke only in impressions. One-Bird was a marvellous mimic. When a passerby tossed coins into his well-worn cap, One-Bird rewarded him with an uncanny impression.

"Oom-tay my la, you dirty rat." An impeccable Jimmy Cagney.

"Ya monto la-pe-ya Cowbells." He had Christopher Walken's halting cadence down pat.

"Lo-farwa been lay, Mr. Freeze." He even did George Clooney! No one did George Clooney!

Every one of One-Bird's impressions was spot on, from

Gene Kelly and Alan Alda to Daniel Day-Lewis and Meryl Streep. He could have made quite a living had he had just a few more English words in his repertoire. Nevertheless, One-Bird's impromptu performances never failed to cheer Billy up. No matter how bad his day, Tommy's John Wayne impression would put a smile on his face.

Billy stopped at the corner and put ten dollars in One-Bird's cap. "How about the Duke? John Wayne."

One-Bird looked at Billy with rheumy, watery eyes and smiled. "Om-pay-la, way bert, Pilgrim."

My God he's good, Billy thought as he smiled back and gave Tommy One-Bird a respectful salute. At the bus stop, Billy bent down to pet a beagle and stepped into a dog turd big enough to be declared a country. Billy looked down at his shoe just as a street cleaner jetted water in a clean arc at his feet, soaking his cuffs.

Well, he thought, at least now my shoes are clean.

On the bus ride over to the Waterhouse building where Dr. Feldman had his office, Billy tried hard not to dwell on the one part of the examination that worried him the most. He was now at that age where the doctor would be examining areas of Billy's body that had never been *examined* before. The Procedure That Must Not Be Named. He didn't want to think about it, but nothing could distract him. Not the crossword puzzle he was working on (24 down: dark cave explorer), not the billboards that flashed past the bus window ("Let your fingers do the walking!"), not even the street signs. Billy had never noticed the corners of Benn and Dover or Probe and Payne before.

Billy squirmed in his seat. There must be a way out of this! No, he corrected himself, this a good thing. Uncle

Roy had been diagnosed with colon cancer at his age, and a family history of the disease increased his chances of having the disease too. Come to think of it, his uncle Roy had been killed in a car crash by a drunk driver immediately after his diagnosis. Uncle Roy had always been the lucky one in the family, Billy thought wistfully. He once won a wok in a charity raffle.

Billy decided not to worry about the exam. It would be over in a second. Procedures That Must Not Be Named happened every day, he reasoned. The secret was to not make it a big deal. For the rest of the bus ride, Billy made a mental list of things to talk to the doctor about during the sure-to-be-awkward part, to make it less so. After all, it couldn't be the highlight of the doctor's day either.

At the corner of Wide and Spread—how could he have not noticed these names before?—Billy rang the bell, then stepped out onto the street and gazed up. Waterhouse Five was one of the most beautiful buildings in town. Twenty-five stories of elegant art deco architecture sat atop a wide portico emblazoned with a large number five in a wonderful terracotta sunburst design. Art deco was Billy's favourite style of architecture, and there weren't many better examples of it in town. Sometimes he came by the Waterhouse just to appreciate its beauty and walk through its majestic interior. To Billy, it was a work of art. For a moment, he forgot himself and his anxiety.

Billy passed through the well-appointed lobby, tripped on his shoelace, and almost molested an eye-poppingly buxom blonde. After a quick and sincere apology, he made his way to the elevators. He pushed the Up arrow, entered the elevator, and pressed 14. Most buildings don't have a thirteenth floor based on some silly superstition, Billy remembered. He guessed the Waterhouse was no exception. But what does it matter, he thought, thirteen or fourteen, misfortune doesn't have a favourite number.

When Billy got to the doctor's office, there seemed to be a crisis of some sort.

"Hello, Mr. Jonah, it's been a while," said the receptionist, Sally. Or was it Sandra?

She looked like a Sandra, but her name was Sally. Some people, Billy thought, are cursed with the wrong name. He always felt a little sorry for them.

"Yes, I guess it has been a while."

"Well, you can just sit down there. We're in the middle of a little disaster. The phone system and the computers are down. You're our last appointment. We probably would have had to close down if this had happened earlier. You're lucky."

Billy smiled warmly. He actually began to relax in the plush waiting room chair. It's all good, he thought to himself, it's all—

"Mr. Jonah?" The sound of the receptionist's voice made him jump.

"Yes?"

"Examination room A, please."

Billy ventured down the corridor, saw the door marked "A," and sat on the examination table inside. Strumming his fingers on the table with a practised nonchalance, he looked around. Nothing unusual. Your basic examination room. Poster of the nervous system on the wall, tongue depressors and lollipops in a glass jar on the desk. His eyes caught the box of rubber gloves sitting beside a tube of lubricant just as Dr. Feldman walked in.

"Billy, long time no see."

"Yes, yes, long time …" Billy had a hard time swallowing.

"Any problems? Anything causing you trouble?"

And just like that, the examination was under way. Family medical history, blood pressure cuff, heartbeat check, abdomen palpated. Everything was going smoothly. In fact, the doctor commented on how optimal Billy's blood pressure and heart rate were for a man of his age.

Then it was time.

"All right, Billy, if you can pull your pants down and lie on your side on the table with your knees drawn up."

"Sure," he croaked. He cleared his throat. "Yes, of course." He unbuckled his belt, pulled down his pants, and lay on the examination table. There was a knock at the door and Sally/Sandra poked her head in.

"I was just going for coffee. Would you like anything?"

"No, but thank you," Billy said.

"Uh … I was talking to the doctor."

Feldman laughed. "No, in fact you might as well go home for the day. You can't do the billing till the computers are back up."

"Lovely, my lucky day. See you tomorrow. Goodbye, Mr. Jonah."

"Uh—yes, bye." Billy had never felt more vulnerable. He hoped the flush in his cheeks hadn't travelled to his … cheeks.

The door clicked closed. As Billy lay on his side, knees raised, staring at the wall, he could hear the snap as Feldman put on the rubber glove. It was not a comforting sound. Billy readied himself with the first topic on his Procedure That Must Not Be Named conversation list.

"Looks like the Leafs may do well this year, huh? The defence looks solid. Maybe just need ..."

But Dr. Feldman wasn't a hockey fan. He didn't care about the Leafs and what they needed, because at that moment he was being professional and concentrating on what he was about to do next. He thought to himself, "Remember to tell Billy what's about to happen," but he was so focused on the job at hand, he forgot. It was an unfortunate turn of events. Had Dr. Feldman reviewed Billy's medical file more closely, he would have noted that Billy suffered from hyperekplexia, an extreme startle response to noises or other disturbances typically found only in babies. Unfortunately for the good doctor, he was disturbing Billy mightily right then, and Billy's hyperekplexia kicked into high gear.

Billy's response was immediate and involuntarily: his knees pushed violently against the wall, propelling his body backward and driving Feldman's finger farther inside him than either Feldman or Billy would have preferred. In agony, Billy gasped and rolled over onto his back, bending Feldman's finger to an impossible angle, breaking it. Feldman cried out. Immediately, his broken finger began to swell.

Billy's rectum clenched in full spasm, firmly trapping Feldman's finger. Off balance and in considerable pain, Feldman fell to his knees, smacking his head into the examination table and knocking himself unconscious. Feldman lay on the floor, his arm raised in the air and his finger firmly plumbing his patient's posterior. Billy lay in shock on the table, feeling more violated than he ever had before. Had anyone walked in at that moment, they would have seen something that looked like a capital *H* fallen on its side.

"Dr. Feldman ... are you all right?" Billy had a feeling that this was a stupid question.

No answer.

It says a great deal about Billy that at this particular juncture, his main concern was for Feldman's well-being. After all, Billy was in a deeply compromising position. He racked his brain for a way to get help for the doctor. He breathed deeply to calm himself and tried to think clearly. Here were the facts as he saw them:

1) He had an unconscious, possibly concussed, medical doctor firmly attached to his ass.
2) There was no one around to hear his cries for help.
3) There were no working phones to make calls and no working computers to send emails.
4) His cell phone was drying out on his bathroom vanity because he'd dropped it in the toilet that morning.

Billy suddenly remembered that his dentist, Dr. Phillips, had an office on the sixteenth floor of the Waterhouse! Now, granted, this was above and beyond a root canal, but Billy surmised the physics were the same. Anyway, at the very least, Dr. Phillips could get help for the unconscious Dr. Feldman. Billy had to try.

Slowly, Billy rolled back onto his side and inch-wormed off the examination table, trying not to hurt either himself or the doctor. He managed to stand, albeit awkwardly, feet apart with the doctor lying between them. He hoped, self-consciously, that the doctor would not regain consciousness at this moment and look up.

Billy jumped up and down, gently trying to dislodge Feldman's finger, but not surprisingly, had no luck. Then he braced his hands on his knees and squatted, relaxing as much as he could. Again, nothing. They'd have to head to the elevator as one. He looked about the room, and noticed the doctor's chair had wheels. It was height-adjustable, and at its lowest setting would be about a foot off the ground. Billy came up with a plan that MacGyver would have been proud of and grabbed the sheet that covered the examination table.

He wound the sheet into a makeshift rope and hung it around his neck. Putting his arms between his legs and grabbing Feldman's free wrist, he pulled the doctor towards the chair. It was hard work, made much harder with his pants around his ankles and the fit of uncontrollable giggles that racked Billy's body when he thought about what he was doing.

When he reached the chair, he adjusted it to its lowest height. He took the sheet from around his neck and looped it around the chair. He pulled Feldman onto the seat and wrapped the sheet tightly around the doctor's waist, securing him to the chair back. He grabbed the end of the sheet and pulled/wheeled the slumped doctor (still firmly attached to him via his finger) out of the examination room and into the hall.

"Sally?" he called, and then thought better of it. "Sandra?" he called a little louder.

No answer.

A thin film of sweat covered Billy now, making him uncomfortable, though not as uncomfortable as having Feldman's slumped head inches away from his crotch. Billy kept hoping that all of this physical activity would pop out the offending finger. Nope.

The worst is behind me, thought Billy without irony. Slowly pulling the doctor along, he made his way to the elevator, looking like a very odd car ornament. Thank God there's no one around to see this, he thought. Maybe his luck was changing. He pushed the Up arrow. Almost immediately the elevator arrived, its carriage empty. Billy got them both inside and pushed the button for the sixteenth floor.

As the elevator rose, Billy felt good. In fact, he felt more than good. He felt invincible. Every difficulty that had come his way this afternoon had been dealt with. And he was moments away from rescue. What could go wrong? Superstitiously, he tried to stop that thought even as it dawned, but it lodged firmly in his brain.

What could go *wrong*? What did I think *that* for? That's the death knell! I've jinxed it! Lots of things could go wrong! Billy took two deep breaths and forced himself to relax. I've already acknowledged the "what could go wrong," he thought. Now I'll be fine.

Billy was still thinking positive thoughts as he shuffled out of the elevator and into the press conference.

The city's oldest practising physician was turning ninety years old today, and there was an enormous civic celebration. Of course, thought Billy—Dr. Phillips's old friend Dr. Hackett! Congratulations were in order, he thought as he spied the old doctor. Then, Billy quickly remembered himself. Thankfully, no one appeared to have seen him yet, and Billy prayed that he could step back into the elevator with the unconscious Dr. Feldman without being noticed.

Ping!

The elevator door closed behind him and pulled on the sheet. Feldman slumped forward onto the floor, his hand raised in mock salute to Billy's ass.

The heads of all the guests and photographers turned towards him. The room fell absolutely silent.

Billy looked plaintively from face to face. Oh, he thought sadly, with his pants around his ankles, *this* is what could go wrong. He managed to speak: "Could someone please give me a hand?"

Some wag from the back shouted, "Looks like someone already did."

The room exploded into laughter.

Two hours later, Billy left his favourite building in the city, its memory forever tainted. Stepping gingerly onto his bus, he noticed that many of the passengers were looking at him. He looked down in a panic, wondering what evidence of his misfortune remained.

A teenager sitting near the front said, "Hey, you're the YouTube guy!"

"What?" Billy asked weakly.

The boy turned his iPad to show Billy. Someone had shot video of him as he emerged from the elevator, capturing every moment clearly in HD.

As he got off the bus and made his way home, Billy reflected with characteristic optimism that it could have been a lot worse. Dr. Feldman was being held overnight to check for symptoms of a concussion, but aside from that, he was expected to make a full recovery. At least no one had died. At least, not yet. Billy still needed to have the examination. He was fifty, after all, and had a family history.

Up ahead, under a lamppost, Billy spied Tommy One-Bird. Well, Billy said to himself, maybe this day will end on a good note after all.

"Hey, Tommy. I've had a bad day. Really, *really* bad. I could use some cheering up. Could I bother you for a John Wayne?" Billy gave One-Bird a twenty-dollar bill. Tommy's eyes lit up. As his mouth opened, Billy was already smiling in anticipation.

One-Bird said to Billy: "Pilgrim Poo-tee-weet?"

'Twas Not Right
Before Christmas

INSPIRED BY CLEMENT MOORE'S
"'TWAS THE NIGHT BEFORE CHRISTMAS"

'Twas the night before Christmas, when all through the house
Not a creature was stirring, not even a mouse.
The stockings were hung by the chimney with care,
When the space–time continuum suffered a tear.

The children were nestled all snug in their beds,
iPod Touch earbuds attached to their heads.
The wife in her jammies retired with tea
While I shoved all the gifts 'neath our fake Christmas tree.

I took a short rest from the holiday cheer,
Grabbed forty winks—woke up craving a beer.
I walked to the kitchen to fetch the cold brew,
And glanced at the clock: 'twas elev'n fifty-two.

In just a few minutes, 'twould be Christmas Day,
But the whole thing felt wrong, in a temporal way—
And not just wrong time, but wrong age and wrong place!
I broke out in a sweat—my heart started to race.

I didn't belong here, of that I was certain.
I dashed to the window to peer through the curtain.
The new-fallen snow sparkled under the stars
My street seemed so different, with odd-looking cars.

I looked at our Bose gear, our flat-screen TV,
Our Blu-ray, our Xbox, PlayStation and Wii.
I knew all their names, all the functions they had,
Yet they all seemed so modern, newfangled—"Egad!"

I said it out loud, a most old-fashioned word,
And yet as I said it, it seemed not absurd.
In fact, it felt natural, at home on my lips
Like "Good golly!" "My heavens!" and "Oh fiddlesticks!"

Something was warped here, ev'n anachronistic:
I belonged to the past, and a life more simplistic!
With mamma in her kerchief, and I in my cap,
My brain should be settled for a long winter's nap.

Instead I was wondering what I should do
As a strange glowing light glided into my view.
The light shimmered shapelessly over the floor,
Floating in space, between me and the door.

The light dimmed a moment, and then I divined
The shape of a man! (Was I losing my mind?)
My mouth slowly opened but ere I could ask,
I heard, "I am the Ghost of All Christmases Past."

I stood there quite stunned, knowing not what to say.
So the Ghost went on blithely since that was his way:
"I will show you your past, where you went wrong in life.
Consumed with your business, ending up with no wife."

"I'm sure that sounds lovely," said I cautiously,
"But there's been a small error—I'm sure you'll agree
When you learn my wife's sleeping upstairs in our bed,
Which is where I should be, but I'm down here instead."

The Ghost looked askance—"Calm down, Ebenezer!"—
Checked a note from his pocket. "Oh, bloody Caesar!
A mistake at Head Office! A grave oversight!
Can they possibly ever get anything right?

I'm not even in London—" as breath he did draw—
I said, "Nope, this is Canada, place called Moose Jaw.
It's cold and remote, with a small population,
But downtown's quite nice, since the 'revitalization.'"

The Ghost smacked his forehead, then took out a map.
Had a look for some minutes, then muttered, "Oh, drat!
I'm not in the right classic nor epoch of time!
I'm stuck midst a wholly wrong holiday rhyme!

"This is highly unusual, confusing, a mess.
Not sure what to do … at a loss, I confess.
Perhaps we should fly to your past anyway?
Straighten things out? Well, what do you say?"

"*You* visit my past. I know it—it's boring.
I'll stay with my family to greet Christmas morning."
This Ghost from the past sent my sense of time reeling.
No wonder I'm caught in this awful strange feeling.

Then out in the kitchen arose such a clatter
I quickly ran in to see what was the matter,
Not sure what I'd find there … A reindeer? A sleigh?
A baby surrounded by cows and some hay?

An old man lay sprawled amid bright pots and pans
Flailing this way and that with his feet and his hands.
He said, "Sorry for coming here out of the blue.
I'm Clarence the Angel and I'm here to help you.

"I'll show you such things as you've never seen.
Like how life would go on if you'd never been."
I replied, "What's the point of this gift you'd bestow?"
That confused him … he whispered, "I don't really know."

The Ghost then decided to enter the fray.
To Clarence he said, "You must share my dismay.
I've attempted to get this man back to the past
But he just won't do anything that I have asked."

Clarence stared at the Ghost, his head gave a sharp jerk:
"You're the Christmas Past Ghost? I'm a fan of your work!"
They dove into shop talk, like old friends at ease,
Till I jumped in, exclaiming, "Hark, gentlemen, PLEASE!

"We three don't belong in the same Christmas tale,
Our three different stories don't really dovetail.
Yet somehow at this point we've all intersected,
I'm baffled, I'm beat—tell me how we're connected!"

The Ghost said, "I'll show you what's really at stake."
The angel said, "I'll show the difference you make."
"Both are good lessons," said I ... sighed and paused.
"I'm in a *fluff* piece about Santa Claus."

"Come with me," Clarence said, "I'll prove and you'll see,
How sad without you your friends' lives would be."
"No, it's me you should come with," the Christmas Ghost bade,
"To see how miserable you are from choices you've made."

"Go get lost, *Casper!*" Clarence swung at the Ghost.
"This guy's coming with me. Back off or you're toast."
The Ghost grew quite angry and kneed a connection
With part of poor Clarence that had no protection.

Clarence bent double; the Ghost jumped on his back.
They fell to the floor—each renewed his attack.
With rolling and brawling, and fighting for glory—
It beat the crap out of a nice Christmas story!

The shocks of the evening had stricken me dumb,
When a small boy appeared; he was sucking his thumb.
My head started throbbing, right up through my sinus.
He snuggled his blanket, said, "Hi, my name's Linus.

"You look quite perplexed, mind all in a whir.
The meaning of Christmas *I'll* tell you, dear sir.
Lights, please," he ordered—like setting the scene—
Then he quoted Luke 2: verses eight to fourteen.

And then things went crazy, they just wouldn't stop—
The house filled with people from bottom to top.
A young boy with glasses ... with Red Ryder gun!
"You'll shoot your eye out—be ... be careful there, son."

Everywhere that I looked was a sight to behold:
A smartly dressed snowman sang "Silver and Gold."
And more were appearing, I saw with frustration,
Some were cartoons, and others claymation.

Small misfit toys climbed up on my shelf.
A runaway reindeer, a blonde dentist elf.
A small drummer boy beat his drum without pause,
Tim Allen in fat suit did his best Santa Claus.

Bing Crosby was singing, a song about dreaming,
And towel-clad M. Culkin kept screaming and screaming.
And there was Bruce Willis, not looking his best,
Yelling, "Yippee ki-yay"—I couldn't make out the rest.

There were birds, there were rings, there were ten lords
    a-leaping.
With such a loud racket, how on earth's my wife sleeping?
I was puzzled and dazed from my head to my socks,
When my living room filled with a blue police box.

Out jumped a tall man with both arms upraised.
"Calm down, take a breath, no need to be crazed!
Things will change back to the way they once were,
That would be best, I'm sure you concur.

"With the help of this gizmo I have in my hand,
I, Doctor Who, will right wrongs, understand?"
"I hate you," said a green man, whose shoes seemed to pinch.
"I'm not that kind of Who, you idiot Grinch."

"What the hell happened?" I asked Doctor Who,
"To cause this confusion, this giant to-do?"
"Can't really explain," he said sheepishly.
"It's too convoluted. Yes, even for me.

"But don't worry, I'll fix it in just half a mo."
He pushed a small button that started to glow.
The Grinch and Bing Crosby and all who'd appeared
Spun around, shrunk right down, and then disappeared!

My home was transformed to what it had been:
I was back in my nightshirt, and all was pristine.
So relieved was I then, I burst into applause,
When I saw by our tree the REAL Santa Claus.

He stood there unsteadily, stroking his beard.
He looked at me blinking and said, "That was weird.
So what should we do, after all that's transpired?"
I said, "Finish up here—I'm really quite tired."

Santa entered the fireplace, climbed up brick by brick,
Shouted back, "Aren't you old to believe in St. Nick?"
"Maybe so," I replied after thinking a bit.
"What I truly believe: I'm too old for this shit."

Santa was shocked. "Why, that was obscene!
It's too bad things are back to the way they had been.
From 'Egad!' and 'Good golly,' you've broadened your scope,
If I'd time I'd be washing out *your* mouth with soap."

Santa got in his sleigh, saying, "Be a good boy.
Clean up your language—earn next year's e-toy."
But I heard him exclaim, ere he drove out of sight—
"Happy Christmas to all, and to all a good night!"

The Grateful Gatsby

INSPIRED BY F. SCOTT FITZGERALD'S
THE GREAT GATSBY

"In my younger and more vulnerable years my father gave me some advice that I've been turning over in my mind ever since."

Eckersley looked at Lord Gatsby expectantly. "And what words might those be, sir?"

"'No matter how dire your predicament, no matter how worrisome your troubles, never be without a shoehorn.'"

Eckersley's brow furrowed. "Please excuse me, sir, but I'm not quite sure I follow."

"I know exactly what you mean. I have no idea what he was on about. But Father did say it whilst on his deathbed and I thought it most impolite to get him to illuminate. It seemed best that he concentrate full bore on the act of dying."

"I believe that was the correct course of action, sir."

"Perhaps it was the correct course." Lord Gatsby sighed. "But was it the prudent one? I sometimes wonder if Father was leaving me a clue as to how to get along in life. You know how fond he was of games. Perhaps it was his last little riddle for me to solve."

"I am sure your father would have come right out and said it. Yes, he did adore his games, but he was not the type of man who would hide something of import in a cryptic saying."

"You may be right, Eckersley. It is just that our recent troubles weigh so heavily on my mind that I feel like a cart in front of the horse with no legs to stand on ... with ..."

Eckersley's eyebrow arched. Lord Gatsby of Beckingham Abbey was a kind and judicious man, but he was not eloquent.

He had just come into the library to see if his lordship had need of anything in particular. In all the years that he had been butler at Beckingham, he could not recall Lord Gatsby spending this much time in the library. Eckersley glanced at the fine writing desk strewn with books on finance and get-rich-quick schemes. Milord is becoming obsessed with his dwindling status, he thought.

The earldom of Gatsby included a title and estate that were the envy of the British Empire. Unfortunately, the last few years had been unkind and the estate was near financial ruin. Gatsby felt a twinge of guilt at the thought that he was glad his dead wife was not here to see this. Although, to be fair, the love of his life, Antoinette LaBoeuferie, was the chief architect of this abattoir of ruin. The beautiful Frenchwoman had an almost obsessive fascination with all things American. She had bought the Brooklyn Bridge no fewer than three times—once when she was in Brussels. Her fascination with fads, expensive fads, soon emptied the Gatsby coffers. But Gatsby could never refuse her anything.

The earl and his bride had enjoyed an unusually happy

marriage and over the twenty years of their union had raised a beautiful daughter.

After Antoinette's death during a faux Fourth of July celebration with spectacularly defective fireworks, the grieving earl went on a spending spree to commemorate her, bringing the family to this horrific precipice of poverty. This seemed to be just the latest in a series of dire events that had Gatsby wondering if the family were cursed in some way. Their misfortunes began five years previous, when his two nephews Jeremy and Tristam died during the sinking of the *Titanic*.

The oddest thing about that disastrous end was that Jeremy and Tristam weren't even passengers on the doomed ship. Always an adventurous pair, they had invented a sport that incorporated ski jumping with North Atlantic iceberg exploration on behalf of the Royal Geographical Society. The location they picked for their maiden attempt was, unfortunately, the offending glacial mass that sunk the great vessel. During a downhill run, they gravely misjudged the slipperiness of the ice (which increased their velocity) and the angle of their trajectory. With cries of "Tallyho!" and "Cheerio!" (meant to chase away their well-founded misgivings), they slammed full tilt into the side of the *Titanic* just as it struck the iceberg. They died instantly. Later, they were counted among the casualties of the sinking by members of the press who thought the true story might bring embarrassment to one of England's most esteemed scientific societies.

That was followed by Gatsby's great-uncle losing his fortune to a Hungarian female impersonator, the divorce of his brother from the Carmichael Hair Tonic heiress, and the deaths of two aunts, a grandfather, both parents, and a beloved Collie named Dora Mae. It was time for things to change. And for that to happen, his daughter, Jane, had to step up to the wicket. If she married advantageously and well, that good connection could be the first step in reclaiming the family's lost stature.

In the last year, Lord Gatsby had considered a number of wealthy suitors for his daughter, but none were, well, suitable.

"I take it Mr. Bentley Fixins-Smythe was not up to snuff?" Eckersley inquired gently.

"Jane thought him a bit of a bore, and rightfully so. He's dreadfully stuffy," the earl admitted. "But sometimes, isn't one bored by the person one loves?"

Eckersley didn't know what to say, but his silence spoke volumes.

"Of course, you are right, Eckersley. What kind of a marriage is that to arrange for my daughter? If I may be totally forthright with you, she is exceptionally picky when it comes to potential suitors. Sir Clayton Morehouse-Finch-Piper is too short, Archibald St. Crispin is too fey, Rupert Bearnum-Haxton has teeth like a can opener. The list goes on."

"If I may say, sir, you don't seem particularly distressed about this latest development in Lady Jane's *affaires de coeur.*"

Lord Gatsby looked around, making sure that they were alone. "My spirits have been buoyed, Eckersley. I have discovered, or more correctly rediscovered, an old romantic interest of Jane's. A chap by the name of Rockefeller Manly. If he proves acceptable, my hope is that he will marry Lady Jane and in so doing, allow us to keep Beckingham Abbey for generations to come."

"That is good news, sir. I must confess, sir, I don't remember the young man. I was certain that I knew all of the young miss's suitors."

"This was before you took employment here, Eckersley. They were four years old."

Eckersley's eyebrows almost rose right off his head.

"Four years old, sir? Does it seem a little optimistic that the spark may still be there? Do you know anything about him?"

"Not a lot, I must say. The last time I saw Rockefeller he was but knee-high to a ... clodhopper? You know what I mean. A most agreeable little chap in short pants. Always smiling, full of intelligent questions, but often content to play quietly with his nanny. A thoroughly delightful young man. But over the intervening years, I'm afraid we lost touch with the Manlys." Gatsby lowered his voice and twisted his moustache. "There was talk of scandal involving his father, a Turkish princess, a Ping-Pong paddle, and a Yorkshire terrier."

Eckersley raised a scandalized eyebrow. "Shocking!"

"Yes," Lord Gatsby exclaimed, "most irregular. For they bred Irish wolfhounds! Heaven knows where the elder Manly got that terrier." He continued. "Rockefeller became an adventurer of sorts, from what I can gather. He seems to have disappeared from public view the last few years. Some say he went to Africa on a goodwill mission, others say India for spiritual guidance. From all accounts, he made a graceful transition from an exceptional child to a remarkable young man. Highly educated, quite handsome, witty, and most important, possibly the saviour of Beckingham Abbey."

Eckersley clucked his tongue appreciatively. "He does sound as though he could be the ticket."

"Indeed. Unfortunately, there are a few hurdles to clear by jumping over them ... so that we can get to the finish ... for a ribbon. First, and this may be the most important task, we have to find him. I have dispatched search parties to Abyssinia and Bombay. I am sure we will turn him up in a few months at the latest. Second, Jane must be persuaded to marry this adventurer. And therein lies the bramble bush that ... ah ... is the ... bush? Blast it all! I am dreadfully unschooled in the construction of colourful metaphors!"

"If you wish, sir, I could prepare a list of metaphors appropriate to a range of situations that might arise."

"Thank you, Eckersley. I have a feeling that we'll be presented with a very delicate situation when we find Mr. Manly, and I shall be in need of it. And if the list makes no mention of bushes, brambly or otherwise, it would be greatly appreciated."

"I think that wise, sir."

Footsteps rang in the hall, and Lord Gatsby's peace was interrupted by a familiar, grating voice.

"Richard! Richard! Are you in the library?" He turned to see his former governess, Mrs. Topworthy, dowager nanny of Beckingham County, stride elegantly but purposefully towards him. At ninety-four years of age, she was still treating him as one of her charges, a habit that had only increased on the death of his parents. He had to admit he still loved it when she read to him.

The dowager nanny fixed her steel-grey eyes upon Gatsby. "I am concerned with the future of Beckingham Abbey and with the happiness of dear Jane. I believe you have a possible husband in mind for her?"

Lord Gatsby's face froze. "What? How did you find out? I only thought of Rockefeller Manly yesterday!"

"My dear boy, if anything ever goes on in this house without my knowing about it, then you can be sure that I'm already in my grave. You're seriously considering Reginald Manly's son?"

"And why would I not? You, more than anyone, have harped continuously about Jane getting married and as soon as possible."

"Yes—but married to a proper husband of spotless reputation. Rockefeller Manly has practically become an American! Though I gather he's made quite a fortune for himself. In women's apparel, I do believe. Can you imagine? Boots and 'leggings,' from what I'm told. They sound shockingly vulgar. I'm afraid he has the taint of the nouveaux riches now."

"Mrs. Topworthy ..."

She pressed a lace handkerchief to her brow. "We shall talk of this later. I'm developing a headache."

"Mrs. Topworthy, wait! I implore you to keep this news to yourself for the time being. At least until I find the fellow and bring him here."

"Very well. Richard, do you need a cardigan? It's getting quite cool."

"No, I'm fine, Mrs. Topworthy. Thank you."

"Are you sure? We don't want you catching cold."

"Quite."

"Well, then, I shall be upstairs resting." She straightened Lord Gatsby's collar and strode from the room.

Lord Gatsby turned to Eckersley. "She's like a dead horse, flogged by a ... Oh drat! You know what I mean ... What is it that I mean?"

"Sir, I believe you were saying, the more cultivated the rose, the sharper the thorns."

"Very good, Eckersley. Very good indeed."

"Father!"

Lady Jane, graceful as a swan, slender as a whippet, contained as a turtle, entered the library. Lord Gatsby was always slightly taken aback by his daughter's beauty. Thank God she took after her mother, he thought. The porcelain skin, the hazel eyes that missed nothing, the silken auburn hair. The sight of her made him ache for his dearly departed wife. The only thing Jane had gotten from her father was her high cheekbones and the upper left side of her forehead.

"Jane! Don't you look radiant!"

"I thought I should make myself presentable should some wayward explorer pop in to marry me and save the future of Beckingham." Jane smiled mischievously.

"Have our private family concerns become the subject of gossip in this house? Dash it all! It was my intention to talk to you of this before it became common knowledge."

"Don't worry, Father. I recognize my duties and obligations as your daughter. Do you think I wish for the loss of our family home and all the goodwill our name has brought to England? I will certainly do my best to entice the young man with my charms and secure an advantageous marriage. I don't know if you've noticed, but

I have raised the hem of my dress to show the ankle of my boot. Do you think I'll be able to attract Mr. Manly with the fine detailing? Being acquainted with boots and leggings and all." She giggled.

"Yes, well, he's not actually in women's clothing." Lord Gatsby paused. "What I meant to say is ..."

"Oh, Father," said Jane with a pout, "I'm not a child. I have actually read some of the books here. I know what a bootlegger is. It makes no difference to me. If it saves the estate, then of course I shall be more than co-operative." She stood on her tiptoes to kiss her father's cheek.

As Lord Gatsby watched his daughter walk away, he spoke to Eckersley, who stood discreetly nearby. "Am I doing the right thing, Eckersley? Perhaps I should have ... oh, I don't know ... gotten a job or something?" He suddenly looked ten years older.

Eckersley raised a sympathetic eyebrow. "Sir, it is the law of the land. Noble families have arranged advantageous marriages for their daughters for centuries. You are doing your duty, sir. Perhaps Lady Jane will discover in doing *her* duty that this young man is pleasing and affection will grow as it should. After all, we do not find love. Love finds us."

Lord Gatsby looked at Eckersley with undiluted admiration. "Well said, Eckersley. Well said."

In the kitchen of the stately mansion, the household staff was uncharacteristically unaware of the slow drama that was unfolding around them. It was lunchtime, and all anyone cared about was eating.

"Thank you ever so much, Mrs. Grimley," said Patsy, the head housemaid, as the cook handed her a sandwich. "No one makes a cheese-and-tomato sandwich like you, and that's no lie."

"The recipe has been in the family for years. It's the secret ingredient that makes it special."

"Which is?"

"No good telling you, my love. Then it wouldn't be a secret ingredient, would it?" Mrs. Grimley cackled. "Everybody happy with the lunch?"

A chorus of "Yes, mums" and "Oh, ayes" sounded from the assembled staff.

"Good. Now if you can spare me for a minute, I'll make me own."

As Patsy dug into her sandwich, she glanced around at the various maids, valets, and other servants seated around the table. This was her favourite time of day. A chance to catch up with the gossip, to commiserate over the workload, to be with her friends. Patsy couldn't remember her life before coming to Beckingham.

Her reverie was disrupted by Jack, the junior groundsman, who burst in from the pantry, chest heaving, forehead beaded with sweat.

"Gaaa ... hurgh ... ledny ... gargg."

Patsy giggled. "Learned a new language, have we? Oooh, you are a bright boy."

"Bloody ... sow!" he gasped. "I'll give you ... a walloping."

"I'd like to see you try. What are you doing back so early? You're not due till later."

Jack looked around the table. "Got a juicy bit of news for you all. I was in town meeting a friend—"

"Oooh," said Iris, an upstairs maid. "The dark-haired one with the full lips?"

"Uh ... yes," said Jack. "Anyway, we were heading to the pub—"

"That friend of yours is very handsome," said Eugenie, a downstairs maid. "Is he married?"

Jack allowed himself a quiet smile. "No, he hasn't found the right woman."

"Nor likely to," Patsy muttered, "if he's anything like your other mates."

"Maybe you could introduce me to him," said Olga, the hound trainer, plucking a pickle from a tray. (Olga wasn't the brightest button in the jar.)

"Which pub did you go to, lad?" asked Rossman, the apprentice valet. "The Groan and Cleaver has an exceptional lunch menu, very reasonably priced."

"Can you all just shut it!" shouted Jack. "This is important!" He waved two letters in the air.

Patsy squinted at the envelopes. "What have you got there, Jack?"

"I ran into Lloyd Sidebottom outside the Spotted Dick. He'd fallen behind on his deliveries, and he asked me to take the post to his lordship."

"Oh," said Patsy, winking. "And I suppose on the way back the envelopes fell to the ground and broke open, and you, being the conscientious junior groundsman that you are, skimmed the letters to make sure nothing was amiss."

Jack smiled sardonically. "Yeah, that's what happened."

He leaned in close to the table and dropped his voice. "The first letter was from Gatsby's barrister in London.

There's a lot of big words thrown about, but the simple meaning of it all is this: Beckingham is almost completely bankrupt!"

Olga crunched her pickle.

Jack continued. "There may be enough for a couple of months, but no more. Which leads me to the second letter. From a possible suitor for Lady Jane."

"Is he rich?" asked Mattingly, the hedge master, whose good eye widened with hope.

"There wasn't a lot in the letter," Jack admitted. "Just that he'd heard the earl was looking for him and that he would drop by in the next week or so."

Patsy chimed in: "Is this the young man the old lady was talking about? The one in women's clothing?"

"Really?" Jack said.

"That's what she said. Boots and leggings, if I remember cor—" Patsy stopped as the realization hit her. "He's a bootlegger!"

"They make a lot of money, don't they?" asked Louise, the chief silver polisher.

"Look, I know as much as you do," Jack said gruffly. "But if Beckingham is in trouble and this Manly doesn't make good, the first to go will be the staff."

"How ... how could they survive without us?" asked Lavin, bathroom oils and salts maintainer.

Patsy looked around the table. "I think the real question is, how will we survive without them? With the war on, positions for household staff in these parts will be few and far between. We'd be as useless as teats on a bull."

"Heavens above!" exclaimed Margot, the weekend

croquet mistress. "I never thought there'd come a day when my services wouldn't be needed."

They finished their luncheon in silence.

Lord Gatsby was reshelving books when Hemmingsworth the groomsman burst into the library, looking quite shaken. Lord Gatsby immediately grew worried. He was of the firm opinion that nothing could shake the large Yorkshireman. He had once watched Hemmingsworth, after being kicked by a horse, set the compound fracture, sew his own torn skin with a bootlace, bind his shattered knee, and then continue grooming the steed as if nothing had happened.

"What is it, Hemmingsworth? A problem at the stable?"

"I believe there is something outside that you should take a look at, sir."

"What is it, man? Spit it out!"

Hemmingsworth looked as helpless as a shorn lamb. He pointed to the door. "Sir, I don't know what it is, but I believe it requires your attention."

When the earl saw what Hemmingsworth was referring to, he had to admit that the groomsman had been in remarkable control of his emotions. There, over the fox and hound topiary on the front lawn, hovered a flying ship. The long, cylindrical body tapered at both ends like a giant cigar. The sound from its engines was monstrous. It came to rest on the front lawn and suddenly all was quiet. Neither a tweet from the birds in the trees nor a bark from the dogs in the kennel moved the still air.

Everyone who had been in the great house seconds before stood outside gaping at the spectacle. Three of the upstairs maids fainted, the charwoman giggled hysterically, and the cook's water broke, though she was not pregnant.

Eckersley moved beside Gatsby. "Should I call the constable, sir?"

Lord Gatsby's handsome head whipped around. "Call the constable? To do what? Toot his whistle at this thing and move it on its way?"

"Forgive me, sir, I panicked."

Jack ran up, breathless. "Sir, do you think it's German?"

"Of course it's German! It's a Zeppelin."

Suddenly a door at the bottom of the vessel opened and a short ramp was lowered to the ground.

The earl turned around, raised his arms, and spoke to the crowd. "All right, everyone! Keep calm! Let us show these Krauts how the British deal with adversity!"

A woman's voice rang out from the back of the crowd. "Are we surrendering?"

Gatsby turned crimson. "Never!" he hollered at the top of his lungs.

"Then why are your arms raised?" called out the voice.

"I raised them to get your attention, you daft woman!"

"You had our attention. Are you sure you're not—"

"Madam, I assure you that we are not surrendering. Just follow my lead."

Eckersley stepped in. "Everyone stay calm and let us preserve the dignity of Beckingham as we face our foes." He turned to Lord Gatsby and lowered his voice. "Sir, if these people have hostile intentions ..."

Gatsby allowed a small smile. "Then I fear the next few moments will be filled with running, screaming, and dying. Prepare to protect our women."

The voice rang out from the back of the crowd. "Look!"

Emerging from the dark interior of the Zeppelin were four men, all of them magnificent, handsome, broad-shouldered chaps with blindingly white smiles.

"Americans!" exclaimed the voice in the back.

One of the four men gave a huge, good-natured laugh. "The name's Sergeant Tex Masterson. We didn't mean to scare ya'll. We're Allies, after all." The sergeant winked at the group, specifically the women. "Appropriated this little German balloon here," he said, slapping the side of the Zeppelin appreciatively. "Just came to drop off something from back home, then we'll be on our way."

Lord Gatsby stepped forward. "Good day, Sergeant. I am Richard Gatsby, master of Beckingham Abbey. We would be honoured to have American members of the Allied forces as our guests—even if it did take you two and a half bloody years to get here. Eckersley, set up the picnic tables for an outside tea."

"Certainly, sir. Jack, Patsy, gather the others and set up a tea service."

The American smiled warmly. "We'll that's mighty kind of you, Dick."

"Richard Gatsby, Earl of Beckingham," he corrected.

"Sure thing, Earl. Well, we didn't just drop in empty-handed. Brought a long-lost acquaintance of yours and an old amigo of mine. Picked him up in Southampton. He tells us he's got a rend-ee-vous with a filly named Jane!"

"Lord Gatsby?" Striding down the ramp was a tall man in a crisp white linen suit. His face, beneath a straw boater, was kind and open with large brown eyes.

Jane, who had ventured out onto the lawn in a pristine

white gown belted with a pale blue ribbon, stood slightly apart from the others with a startled expression on her lovely face. When she recovered from her surprise, she masked her features with feigned indifference, but her cheeks bloomed pink and betrayed her.

The tall man shook the earl's hand firmly.

"Rockefeller? Rockefeller Manly! Good lord, I haven't seen you in years and yet—and yet I'd know you anywhere. Why didn't you tell me you were coming?"

"I did. I sent you a letter as soon as I heard you were looking for me."

"Um ..." Jack stepped forward. "Mr. Sidebottom just gave me these to give to you, milord." He handed Gatsby the two letters. Gatsby glanced at them.

"Damn war, I suppose. Really playing havoc with the postal system. Oh well, you're here and that's the important thing." Gatsby clapped Manly heartily on the back and guided him along the gravel drive to where Jane stood.

"I am delighted to find such a warm welcome from such a beautiful family." Manly stood before Jane and smiled appreciatively.

"Rockefeller, my daughter, Lady Jane. If I'm not mistaken, you were adoring playmates at the age of four or so."

"I'm sure Mr. Manly would not remember that," Jane said demurely, gazing at her white shoes.

Manly's eyes, filled with amusement and something far more exciting, locked onto Jane's. "I assure you, Lady Jane, I could never forget you. Especially not your skill at tiddlywinks!"

Jane laughed becomingly. "I think I shall check and see how they're getting along with the tea. Please excuse me.

It is a rare pleasure to see you again." She curtsied prettily and walked across the lawn to the main garden.

Gatsby slapped Manly on the shoulders. "You have no idea how glad I am that you're here! You're a soothing balm for eyeballs that have become tired through ... for the ... Harrumph." Lord Gatsby coughed with embarrassment. "Do come into my study for a moment before tea is served. I'd like to make a proposal."

When they emerged from the study twenty minutes later, Lord Gatsby's lips were set in a grim line.

The earl said little as he watched Jane preside over afternoon tea. The letter from his barrister had dampened his high spirits. At least we have tea, he thought. Life is so much easier to face when one has tea.

The impromptu party was, of course, a resounding success. The American visitors, though a tad rough around the edges, were unfailingly polite and conducted themselves with complete propriety. They seemed to enjoy the watercress sandwiches and Cook's gooseberry scones and clotted cream. After, at Lord Gatsby's urging, Eckersley and Jack led the servicemen on a tour of the estate. Jack, in particular, seemed very happy to show the Yanks a good time.

Gatsby, Manly, and Jane watched as the men walked down the gravel path to the stables. Lord Gatsby turned to Rockefeller. "Perhaps you could tell Lady Jane of your adventures abroad?"

Rockefeller smiled. "I suppose I can give you the condensed soup, so to speak. I believe the last time I saw you, it was at the tender age of six."

"You had just turned seven," Jane said. "We had a

birthday party and I gave you a little wind-up clown." Rockefeller smiled a wondrous smile, the warmth of which took Jane quite by surprise. "At least that's what I recall." She returned his smile. "But it was a long time ago."

"I believe you're right, Lady Jane. Shortly after my seventh birthday, my father became ambassador to Turkey and my life as a nomad began. More foreign posts followed, and I learned to love travel. As a young man, I was filled with wanderlust and a curiosity about other peoples and cultures. Wherever I went, I made a point of learning about the latest advances in local technology and in the sciences. In the Orient I even dabbled in mysticism and the power of the mind. I never stayed in one place very long. Shortly after the war started, I found myself in New York. Dabbled in a little start-up and made a lot of money."

"Oh, that's when you ... entered the refreshment business?" Jane euphemized.

Rockefeller, catching Lord Gatsby's stern eye, smiled uncomfortably. "Yes. But I'm not in that line of work anymore. Turns out the government discourages that sort of thing. I'm afraid I have no great fortune left. Does that disappoint you?"

"Oh. I ... Well, that is to say ..." Jane looked questioningly at her father.

"My dear, Mr. Manly and I have spoken at length about his circumstances. And though he possesses less in the way of material wealth than we had supposed, he does possess that which makes a marriage most advantageous." He paused dramatically. "He is the sole male heir to the Manly Sporting and Gaming empire. A marriage will give us the means to ensure that the estate remains in the family and is settled upon your firstborn son ... Should you wish to ... enter into ... That is to say ... matrimonially speaking ..." Lord Gatsby coughed and looked away.

"I see," replied Jane primly.

"Lady Jane, do not be too disappointed. I'm a great catch, as New Yorkers say. I'm a little full of myself at times, but no more than the average man. And I have many talents. I throw amazing parties, can dance the tango, I juggle oranges, and I can cook too." He gave her a dazzling smile.

"We have a cook," Jane replied tartly.

Rockefeller laughed good-naturedly. "And a fine cook you have. Jane, I just want to make you happy. After all my years of roaming, I want to settle down and have a family."

"But why did you never settle down in America? The women there are lovely, I'm sure. Forthright and unencumbered by class distinctions, I suppose." Jane's tone had grown a little petulant.

"They are, but I'd prefer an English rose to an American daisy."

"I agree!" said Lord Gatsby. "Anyone can pluck a daisy, but an English rose requires care to get past the inevitable pricks ... of the thorny parts ... those pricks."

Rockefeller beamed a devastating smile at Jane. "Thankfully, I have a green thumb."

"Well," Jane said, not realizing how husky her voice had grown, "we'll have to see how that turns out."

Lord Gatsby had a feeling he knew exactly how it would.

The sun was casting long shadows across the garden when Sergeant Masterson announced that it was time for the Yanks to leave. Even Mrs. Topworthy, the dowager nanny, was sad to see them go.

"They're so sweet!" she announced by way of explanation when Gatsby noticed the twinkle in her eye. "I cannot help but find them charming." She leaned into his shoulder. "And physically, they're quite superior to British men."

"Mrs. Topworthy!"

"Just because there's snow on the roof, doesn't mean you can't blow in the furnace," she insisted. "Where's your hat?" she said, eyeing Gatsby's ruffled hair. "You'll catch a cold."

Lord Gatsby joined Manly, who was saying goodbye to his friends. Tex actually looked as though he might cry. "Manly! Nice to catch up, short as it was." He turned to Lord Gatsby. "Don't know what we'll do without this fella!"

"Tex, there're two barrels of whiskey left in the hold," Manly said, clasping Tex's arm.

"Well, we appreciate your contribution to the war effort, old sport!"

The Americans boarded their vessel. With a mighty roar, the engines ignited and the airship rose, flying off into the sky, disappearing from view an hour and forty-five minutes later.

Everyone went inside, leaving Jane, Lord Gatsby, Rockefeller Manly, and Eckersley on the lawn.

Jane was the first to speak. "I suppose we should get you set up in one of the guest bedrooms."

Manly looked first at her, then at her father. Lord Gatsby nodded.

"Jane, my love, I hope to be here forever. I've been talking with your father about a truly wonderful modern idea I have. It could be just the ticket to a new fortune!" They headed into the house, arms linked.

"Do you know of this grand idea, sir?"

"I do, Eckersley. My late wife would have been fully behind it. My father too, come to think of it. Well, what does it matter? As they say, necessity is the parent of having to do what must be ... done ... in order to have that which ... I'm going to lie down for a while."

Lord Gatsby left Eckersley alone on the lawn and walked slowly towards the great spires of Beckingham Abbey.

Three months later, on a bright sunny day in August, Lord Gatsby glanced at his checklist. "Eckersley, do we have enough shoehorns for this afternoon's festivities? The Ladies' Auxiliary is scheduled to arrive momentarily."

"I assure you, sir, all is in readiness. Each lady will have a freshly polished shoehorn. The preparations have gone swimmingly."

"Hmm. Perhaps Father was on to something after all. A shoehorn certainly has become a necessity around here." Lord Gatsby looked around at the once glorious ballroom of Beckingham. It still took him by surprise that this enormous room had been converted into a nadir of American athleticism. But in truth, it had not taken much to transform one to the other: the parquet floors glowed with polish, and at the end of the hall, Lord Gatsby had added a trophy case with his cricket ribbons, his daughter's various tennis and elocution awards, and his wife's dance trophy. "Do you still find all of these changes difficult to get used to, Eckersley? Or am I the only one in the household whose feet are stubbornly rooted in the soil of the past?"

"I apologize for mixing metaphors, sir, but it seems that since the war started, we are all adrift in the wake of change."

"Nicely said, Eckersley."

"Thank you, sir. Some may see these events as progress, but I must confess, sir, I long for the old days when Beckingham was your home and sanctuary and not a place of frivolous entertainment." Eckersley arched a disapproving eyebrow and glanced with undisguised distaste at the whirring cotton candy machine.

"Well, to be fair, Eckersley, Mr. Manly kindly and quite generously invested in this new chapter of Beckingham Abbey. Without his assistance, our family's legacy would be lost." He gestured widely. "This was the only way to keep both in the family." He paused. "Antoinette would have loved the idea. But, of course, she loved everything to do with the States. Will Mrs. Maxwell ever forgive her for that roller skate debacle in the Great Hall? I think not. But skid marks aside, I think that even you must admit that our first few months have been very successful. And there has been talk of expanding the franchise to London and other cities. I do believe that all will turn out well." Lord Gatsby clasped his hands behind his back and surveyed the ten regulation lanes that stretched the length of the room beneath an enormous crystal chandelier.

"Yes, milord, I suppose that soon all of Europe will be talking of Beckingham Alleys. Now, will Lady Jane be joining the rest of the ladies in the festivities?"

Lord Gatsby smiled at the name of his daughter. "I certainly hope so. Her new husband will be quite put out if she doesn't."

At the end of each of the ten lanes that made up Beckingham Alleys, members of the earl's staff worked feverishly. Some were not enamoured of their latest duties. Jack, the junior groundsman, was especially peeved. Polishing what seemed like his millionth bowling pin, he complained to all who would listen, while a cigarette dangled precariously from the corner of his mouth.

"I'm a *groundsman*, bigod! Bloody 'ell! I'm tired of making these pins shine, I'm tired of polishing the balls of every Tom, Dick, and Harry that walks through the bloody door!"

"That's the first time you've ever complained about that, I'm sure," said Patsy. "But I dare say you could learn a thing or two about making pins shine." She raised her skirts to reveal an ankle swathed in thick flesh-coloured stockings. "Fancy my 'ladies' apparel'?" She snorted with laughter.

"You might want to be careful how you talk, Patsy. Right now, I'm a lowly groundsman, forced to do menial chores. But one day ... you just watch out."

Patsy smiled. "I am watching out, Jack. You've gone from groundsman to balls polisher. And, my oh my, it only took you two years. Who knows, in another year or so, you could work your way up to downstairs pantryman." She chuckled to herself. "Look, no one's happy about this arrangement, Jack. Why can't you just make the best of it? The bowling alley has brought more than a nice little penny to the coffers of Beckingham, which can only benefit all of us. I notice you weren't complaining when the men's Olympic swim team dropped by for a quick dip and a bowl. No, you were more than a little giddy that day."

Jack reddened to the colour of an overripe tomato. "I want to be a doctor's assistant! That's why I study men's anatomy!"

"Of course. You and Mrs. Topworthy!"

"Keep it down over there!" intoned Mrs. Maxwell. The housekeeper was making the rounds, keeping check on her charges. "This is neither the time nor the place for rowdiness. We might be toiling in a bowling alley but that doesn't mean we forget ourselves or our positions in this noble household. We are the backbone of the finest home in England. Do you not agree, Mr. Carlyle, Miss Fenster?"

Patsy and Jack mumbled as one. "Yes, Mrs. Maxwell."

"Let us concentrate on the job at hand, shall we? The Ladies' Auxiliary will soon be here. Now, where's Dottie?"

Patsy pointed to the concessions stand. "She's helping Mrs. Claymore with refreshments. They were having some trouble with the poached salmon and mousseline sauce. But it looks like Dottie has slapped the mousse in line."

Jack groaned.

Mrs. Maxwell scowled. "Patsy, you know his lordship's views on puns! You know better."

Patsy lowered her eyes. "Yes, mum." It took all her strength not to say something about a fair pun-ishment.

The Ladies' Auxiliary arrived promptly at two. The auxiliary consisted of twenty women ranging in age from twenty to seventy, some married, some unattached, some more than pretty, some less than attractive. The only thing they had in common was their considered opposition to progress of any kind. Any new idea expressed through books, music, art, fashion, philosophy, or philanthropy was staunchly belittled, besmeared, and besmirched. The auxiliary's success rate for stanching the flow of progress was poor at best, but it didn't dampen their spirits. Lord Gatsby expected that quite a number of the ladies visiting today would be sure to give voice to their disapproval of the renovations to the ballroom. That is, until he heard bursts of giggles and titters of anticipation at the bowling lanes.

Eckersley and two other servants handed out shoes at a fevered pace. The ladies bustled about, hiking up their stockings, squeezing into the shoes, and dividing themselves up into teams. To Lord Gatsby's surprise and delight, their excitement was positively cacophonous. Their enthusiasm certainly made up for any deficiencies in their talent. From the two-handed-toss-between-the-legs to the one-handed-throw-to-the-gutter, the event was a cornucopia of styles, grace, and talent.

Everyone was having a jolly time, not counting the staff, who whilst resetting the pins, dodged wayward bowling balls dispatched by the more vigorous ladies of the auxiliary.

"Bloody 'ell!" cursed Jack. "Why are they taking their turns before we've set the pins? Sodding clueless uppercrust cows." A ball thudded into his ankle, and he swore viciously.

"Sorry!" trilled the pasty-faced matron who had launched the missile, a big smile on her face.

"You should get your picture taken when you're sorry," Jack muttered.

"Keep your voice down!" Patsy hissed. "Do you want to lose your job?"

"Yes! Yes, I want to lose this job! I can't believe I'm about to say this, but I miss cleaning up after the dogs in the gardens. I tell you, Patsy, if there was anything out there that was even close to being better than this job, I'd be out of here before you could say Jack Sprat."

"And I keep telling you, Jack, if you opened your eyes and saw how good you have it at Beckingham, you'd be a better person for it. And less miserable, too, I wager. Or perhaps you'd rather be on the battlegrounds of France with bullets flying about that lump of pudding you call a head."

Jack was about to retort when a bowling ball bounced off the lane and hit him square in an area that didn't take kindly to being hit square in.

"Aaaaiaaie!"

"Sorry! My fault again. So sorry," came the high-pitched apology.

Jack glared at the Ladies' Auxiliary with undisguised hate. One day, he thought, one day I will be above you all.

Lord Gatsby grudgingly admitted to himself that he enjoyed the sights and sounds of this frivolity. Too often of late, gloom and doom had cast the country in a pall. The fickle fortunes of the world war had brought everyone in England down. It pleased him to feel that he was doing something for his country's morale. A small thing, this bowling alley, but it brought happiness, which was vital.

And now that the fortunes at Gatsby had turned around with the marriage of Jane and Rockefeller, there was joy in his household again.

Lord Gatsby's reveries were interrupted by a familiar voice.

"I have recently acquired membership in the Ladies' Auxiliary, Richard. I find that they are against a great many things that I too am leery of. Did you know there are a number of parliamentarians who don't wear sock garters? With society falling about our ears, keeping your socks up is a step in the right direction." Mrs. Topworthy glanced around with undisguised disapproval. "I did not think my first outing with these esteemed ladies would take place here at Beckingham. Trust the Americans to take a lovely little outdoor pastime and cram it indoors. And why must everything be so grotesquely large?" She squinted down the lanes at the pins erected at the end.

"Mrs. Topworthy, wait!" Lord Gatsby handed her a pair of shoes and lowered his voice. "You cannot step onto the playing area in your street shoes. Wear these."

"I have never worn street shoes in my entire life, Richard," she trilled. Nonetheless, she reluctantly took the shoes he proffered, examining them with pronounced distaste.

Lord Gatsby slapped his forehead at his oversight, grabbed the shoe spray off the counter and gave the inside of each shoe a generous coating. "There," he said, relieved, "all disinfected and ready to go."

"I do hope it is the shoes to which you refer, Richard." The dowager nanny raised her dainty chin and made her way over to her new friends.

Eckersley appeared at Lord Gatsby's elbow. "Sir, 'tis a lovely sight, indeed, to see friends and family enjoying themselves so much."

"It would be hard to disagree with you, Eckersley. It was most fortunate that we made a reconnection with our friend. Funny when you think of it. Rockefeller, Jane's first love, travelled the world, exposed himself to new adventures and cultures, and had the opportunity to make his life anywhere. Yet he came back here to help us and claim Jane for his wife. He brings a game from the United States—my wife's one obsession. It's as though she's still here with me. I suppose no matter how progress ... how far we progress ... that we ... there will ... that is ... Oh, for God's sake! Help me out, Eckersley!"

Eckersley raised an amused eyebrow. "Perhaps this is what you are trying to say, sir. No matter how strange our present and future might appear, we are rooted in what has come before. **So we beat on, boats against the current, borne back ceaselessly into the past.**"

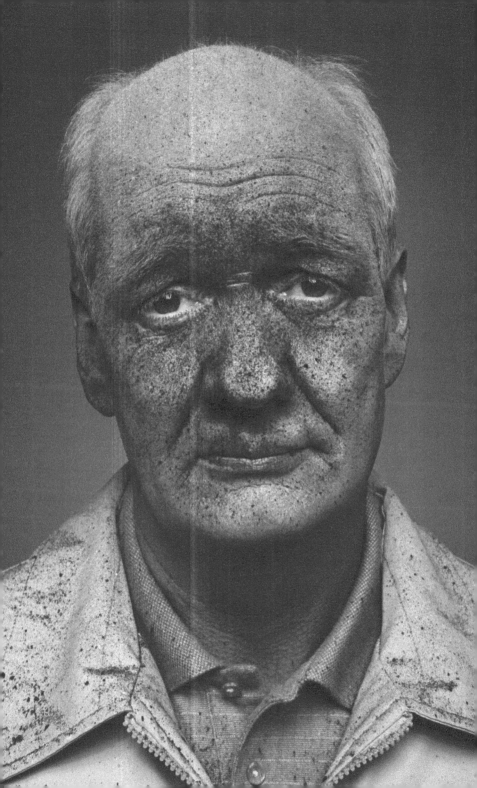

Re: Becker

INSPIRED BY DAPHNE DU MAURIER'S
REBECCA

MONDAY, SEPTEMBER 3

Last night I dreamt I went to Manderley—again. That's six days in a row with the same dream. It's bloody frustrating and bloody boring, I don't mind telling you. Maybe it will all sort itself out when I actually meet Manderley this afternoon. I made the mistake of mentioning the dream at work. Walters in New Foods says that it's a premonition. I said it can't be a premonition, since the dream isn't forewarning anything, except for a meeting that I had already scheduled. Then it's a déjà vu, said Matthews in Baby Food. Déjà vu is the illusion of having previously experienced something actually being encountered for the first time, I said. I haven't met Manderley for the first time, so how can I have a déjà vu? Walters retorted: Well, maybe it's a premonition of a déjà vu. Don't be so bloody literal. Blimey! Don't you have an imagination?

I wonder if every workplace is as barmy as the All Foods Test Laboratory. Or could it be we're all daft from allergic reactions to the foods we sample? Matthews and Walters (two wankers of epic proportion) got one thing right: I have no imagination. But that's probably for the best since my job is to taste and to test dog food. I don't *want* to imagine what such employment has done to my palate, and frankly, having an imagination wouldn't serve me well. My work deals with science and facts. I devise mathematical and chemical formulas to determine moisture, salt content, solubility, and sediment in dog food. My highly trained taste buds can tell the difference between Mr. Mutts Chicken Tasties for Senior Dogs and K-9's Poultry and Sweet Potato Hash for Adult Dogs. Facts and science have been very good to me, so what do I need with an imagination?

Anyway, it's off to Manderley, Austen, and Fishwick, Barristers-at-Law, to conclude a last piece of business for my dearly departed chum Ian.

TUESDAY, SEPTEMBER 4

Although it has been a month since Ian passed, there have been times I've forgotten, and picked up the phone to call him. I suppose it was the suddenness of it all that has made his death so hard to fathom. Well, sudden for us who knew Ian, not so much for Ian himself. He knew he was dying, but chose not to share it with anyone. That one so connected to his chums could carry such a burden alone fills me with complete and utter sadness.

The meeting with Manderley was unusual, to say the least. I drove to his office building, a modern concrete mid-rise in a nondescript office park. His secretary, a pleasant brown-haired woman with round cheeks, welcomed me at the door and offered tea. I refused. I can't drink liquids when I meet someone for the first time: I become hyperaware of the sound of my own swallowing.

Manderley's secretary seemed a bit put out. I did accept a biscuit, which seemed to placate her.

Manderley, who was seated behind his desk when I entered, stood up to shake my hand. "Mr. Morley, so nice to meet you. I wish it could be under more pleasant circumstances."

I looked out the window. "Quite a lovely day for September, though."

Confusion flitted across Manderley's face. "I meant Mr. Becker's passing."

"Yes, of course."

He beckoned me to sit down. I folded my hands in my lap.

"I take it you found the office with no trouble," Manderley said by way of small talk.

"Yes." (Small talk has never been one of my strengths.)

"Well," Manderley said, obviously flustered, "let's get down to it, shall we? Mr. Becker was fairly well off. His comic books—"

"Ian preferred the term 'graphic novels,'" I interrupted.

"What's the difference?"

"About five pounds an issue, I should think."

"Well, no matter the terminology, they sold quite successfully. Throw in the movie adaptations, the merchandising, and such, and Mr. Becker made a nice living." Manderley looked at me, expectantly.

I smiled blankly, waiting for him to finish.

"He wasn't married and he had no heirs. No family at all, as I am sure you know. He had many friends, but it seems you were the one dearest to his heart." Manderley paused dramatically. "He has left his entire fortune to you, Mr.

Morley. A nice tidy sum totalling sixty-five million pounds. In addition, he has left you Becker House, his primary residence in Warwickshire, and his summer residence in the Cotswolds." He eyed me meaningfully over his spectacles.

"Very generous of him. Thank you for letting me know." I got up and made to leave. But Manderley stopped me.

"Sixty-five million pounds, man. That's a lot of money." His eyes widened, and he seemed to be waiting for something.

I cleared my throat. "Yes. It is a lot of money."

"Actually, there's more. Though you have the money, free and clear, he did make a final request."

"Well then, of course, I will do it for him."

"You may change your mind once you have heard it. It is"—Manderley cleared his throat—"highly unorthodox."

"Unorthodox or not, I'll do it. I'll grant his final request. It would seem rather churlish if I didn't."

Manderley didn't respond. He gestured to a wooden box sitting on a table next to a large window overlooking the car park. It was roughly the size of a large jewellery box. It looked quite solid, mahogany, I think, judging by the colour. Each side was covered in a carving of one of Ian's characters: Busy Beaver, the Warlington Strangler, Larry the Literal Man, and Ben-Bop Tweedleham. "Inside that box are Mr. Becker's ashes."

"Seems like a bloody big box for someone's ashes," I said.

Manderley picked up a large plastic bag from behind the desk. "There's more of Mr. Becker in this. People are often surprised at the volume of their loved ones' remains. It's generally more than you would imagine. And the mortician said Mr. Becker's ashes were unusually plentiful. He elaborated with an unnecessarily graphic detailing of the cremation process that I won't repeat." Manderley lowered his voice conspiratorially. "If I can give you a small piece of advice, never talk shop with someone in the death business. They'll tell you stories that would make a goat vomit." He straightened his tie, and when he spoke again it was in a more formal tone. "Mr. Becker has bequeathed his earthly remains to you."

I tried to think of an appropriate place to keep them. My mantel, perhaps, or the sunny spot on the top of the piano? Of course, the plastic bag would fail to blend with my decor. Perhaps I could upgrade to a bigger container.

"As you probably know, the deceased usually requests that their ashes be spread somewhere meaningful. A holiday spot, the place they fell in love, or even a treasured private garden." Manderley paused again. "Mr. Becker's assignation of his mortal remains is quite different. Quite different, indeed."

Manderley opened his desk drawer, took out a manila envelope, and pushed it towards me. "Inside this envelope are the contact details of six people whom Mr. Becker felt had done him some injustice. He has requested that you meet with these people individually and ... throw his ashes into their faces. Their eyes, if possible."

"Righto," I said.

Manderley stared at me. "Did you understand me correctly?" he asked, incredulous. "You are to take Mr. Becker's ashes ..."

"And throw them into the faces, preferably the eyes, of six people. Yes, I believe I have it."

Manderley stared at me, gobsmacked. "I have to say, Mr. Morley, I was expecting an entirely different reaction."

"Like what?" I asked.

"Well … I suppose … any number of reactions, really. Shock, surprise, disgust."

Manderley's disapproval was palpable, and I felt compelled to explain myself.

"Mr. Manderley, Ian is—was—my dearest friend. In fact, he was my only friend. We met when we were twelve. Ian was being bullied by a schoolyard thug, and since I was taller than most of my classmates, I intervened."

"And saving him led to a lifelong friendship? How marvellous."

"No, we bonded on the way to the hospital. I was plucky but uncoordinated and weak. I was beaten like an egg, and Ian walked me to the infirmary. By the time my bruises healed, we were firm friends. We were confidants; we were allies against the world. Ian would have done anything for me, and I, him."

"Well then," Mr. Manderley said, smiling warmly, "I suppose he chose wisely. But I have to say *I'm* still shocked at this. In my dealings with Mr. Becker, he never showed a predilection for revenge, he never struck me as a vindictive man. He was always very charming, quite lovely in fact. He remembered my birthday, and few clients do, I can assure you. Always a Christmas gift for me and Mrs. Wilkens out there." He remembered something, and looked at me, alarmed. "Did you accept her offer of tea?"

"No," I confessed, "but I did take a biscuit."

Manderley looked relieved. "That should be fine, then. As I was saying, Mr. Becker seemed the easygoing sort. The only thing he was ever rigid about was this codicil."

"Obviously it was important to him. So I will honour his wish, and he will not be disappointed." I stopped for a moment. "Although, being dead, I suppose he will not be anything. So ... six people, you said. Depending on their relative proximity, I suppose I could get it done in four weekends."

"Why week*ends*?" Manderley asked, looking up from his papers.

"Why, weekdays are impossible because of work."

"You're going to keep your job?" Manderley asked, quite astonished. "You're a millionaire. You never have to work again."

"I hadn't thought of that." Could I get through the rest of my days without formulating and testing pet food? Yes, I realized, I could, and quite happily too. I took out a notepad. "I had better write this down. *No ... job*. Now, what else should I do, do you think? What would you do if you had sixty-five million pounds, Mr. Manderley? I can't imagine what to do with that much money. Do you have any suggestions?"

I sat poised, my pen in the air.

Manderley stared at me over the enormous plastic bag and wiped a speck of dust from his desk.

WEDNESDAY, SEPTEMBER 5
Today I quit my job. Old Perkins scowled and said that it was actually better for the firm that I was leaving. It's totally untrue, of course, for who else has my grasp of the perfect ash/protein ratio, but Perkins is a bloody fool.

He's on the top of the list for my own ash scattering. Right between his trouty little eyes.

SATURDAY, SEPTEMBER 8

One of the few things I am good at is planning. Given the importance of Ian's final request, I want to make sure that its chances for success are quite high. I am fortunate, indeed, given Ian's extensive travels, that the six people who wronged him are not scattered across the world. One of the six is dead. Four of the remaining five are still in the U.K. Two reside directly in London, and two others are within a three-hour drive. The contact information for the fifth seems to be out of date. But since I now have unlimited funds, I suppose I can hire a private detective to find him.

I can do the first four in six days, including travel time if I opt for a leisurely pace. Three days if I rush and double up on the two in London. I think the more relaxed approach might be nice. Since I am now rich, I could certainly take advantage of the time and make a vacation out of it. After this job is done, I may go abroad for a while. I've never been outside of London in my life. I have never taken a plane. So many firsts to look forward to! Of course, this will also be the first time I've ever thrown the ashes of a friend into someone's eyes, but I'm fairly positive I'm in the majority there.

The dead one is a Mrs. Bernice Lafontaine. I remember her, actually. She brazenly stole Ian's father from his mother, and she was quite despicable to Ian on the days his mother didn't have custody. I'm happy her death was ignoble.

Bernice was a world-renowned unicyclist, and on the

day of her death, attempted to become the oldest cyclist
to cross the Thames on a tightrope. She also would have
been the *only* cyclist to cross the Thames on a tightrope,
but I digress. Unfortunately, she was absolutely bladdered.
Stinking of gin, and flashing antique bloomers, she fell from
her tightrope at midpoint over the river and plummeted
head first into a speedboat full of German tourists. Good
riddance, I say.

As I was poring over the tube maps and circling the
appropriate stations to compile my itinerary, I realized that
I should probably practise my ash-throwing technique.
I'm fairly certain that there are no manuals to study, so
it was incumbent upon me to come up with a competent
method. I set up my dartboard and stuck a page torn from
a magazine upon it. It was a picture of Simon Cowell. I don't
have any particular animosity towards the man, but it was
the only life-sized headshot I could find.

The first thing I discovered was that throwing ashes
accurately is next to impossible. I had to be right on top
of my victim if I were to have any chance of hitting his
face, never mind his eyes. And I was determined to get the
eyes as per Ian's request. I also learned that there could
be no windup. Try standing a foot away from a target and
throwing a ball at it. You naturally follow through, which
means you end up with scraped knuckles or a sprained
wrist. Another impediment: I tend to have sweaty palms.
Which means that more of Ian sticks to me than to
the corneas of my target. And then one must take into
account wind conditions, the height of the victim, etc.
What a messy, complicated business. But I'm determined
to get it right.

I spent the evening sweeping up all the bits of Ian that I had practised with and collected them in a little plastic baggie. Tomorrow, I will pick up latex gloves.

SUNDAY, SEPTEMBER 9

The gloves work like a charm. I practised all day, until I could hit Simon Cowell nine out of ten times. I devised a simple flicking motion that guarantees a high success rate. I am very, very pleased with my progress.

According to the posh-sounding weather lady, it is supposed to rain for the next couple of days, so I will embark upon my journey on Tuesday. I am starting to get excited.

MONDAY SEPTEMBER 10

I watched *Terminator 2* on the telly today. I quite enjoy movies and television. I think it's because the endings always take me by surprise. (Except for the series *Columbo*. You know who the murderer is right away, and you know he's going to get caught by the strange little man. What is the point, I wonder? And which is his good eye?) At one point in the film the Terminator says, "*Hasta la vista*, baby!" Although it sounds ridiculous in an Austrian accent, nevertheless it became a popular catchphrase. I wonder why the supercomputer of the future made his killing machines with barely understandable European accents? No matter. What occurred to me, though, was that perhaps I should prepare a little catchphrase to shout out once I've thrown Ian's ashes into the eyes of my victims.

"Hasta la vista" might be appropriate as I run away from the scene, but I would really like to be able to deliver a pronouncement of sorts, something with *gravitas* that explains the reason for my actions. After hours of pondering my options, the best I could come up with was: "Ian Becker's ashes in your eyes, sucka!" (I added "sucka" to give it more street feel, but I confess the whole phrase seems a little too forced. It's not my style, and it certainly wasn't Ian's.)

I have printed out some famous catchphrases that I hope to adapt to my needs. I find I have really warmed to my task!

TUESDAY, SEPTEMBER 11

I feel as if I am about to embark on a momentous journey. Today, by honouring my dear friend's final wishes, I'm travelling to places I've never ventured to. I'm engaging in behaviour that I'd never previously even considered. I may even be committing crimes. The thought emboldens me.

After wolfing down the largest breakfast I have had in years (two eggs over easy, bacon crisp, four link sausages, pancakes, berries, yogourt, two slices of whole-wheat toast, granola, two cinnamon buns, a chocolate croissant, orange juice, and a pot of coffee), I am heading out with the address of my first target in hand.

LATER, TUESDAY, SEPTEMBER 11

Jeanine Carson. Of the five remaining, she lives closest to me and I know her well. She deserved the fate that Ian had chosen for her. She had married Ian shortly after we graduated from college. From the start it was an unfortunate union. I had tried to warn Ian away from her, but succeeded only in causing a rift in our friendship.

During their short union, Ian and I rarely saw each other. She disapproved of my disapproval.

Now, I am not often subject to bouts of intuition ("gut instincts," as the colonials say), but from the day I first met Jeanine on the campus common, I took an instant dislike to her. Perhaps people who lack certain qualities, like imagination, are more sensitive to the gaps in others' personalities. Yes, I find it hard to dream, to imagine a wide spectrum of possibilities, but in my defence, I submit that I am *fundamentally* a good person. I have common sense, I tend not to judge people, I am a steadfast friend. Not to toot my own horn, but I also have a very low cholesterol count and have been told on more than one occasion that I am an exceptional kisser. Jeanine had lots of dreams and ideas but no common sense, no strong character to anchor her. And in Jeanine's world, she was the main bunny, it was all about her. She was sharp-tongued, selfish, self-involved, and vain. Worst of all, she pronounced "nuclear" incorrectly.

She was breathtakingly beautiful, of course, with auburn hair and deep blue eyes. But Ian would have been happy with someone who looked like a rhino. He was never shallow and certainly not obsessed with physical beauty. I suppose they must have had some things in common, but I can't imagine what. (Not surprising.) It was *her* failings, I was quite sure, that destroyed her marriage to Ian. I saw how hard he worked to make her happy. Marrying her was one of the few lapses of judgment that I could recall Ian ever having.

I know he realized it early on, too. At the wedding, as Jeanine walked down the aisle, he whispered to me, "What have I done? Quick, get me to the car!" Unfortunately, I had a horrendous head cold that impaired my hearing. I thought he said, "You know what'll be fun? Recite me some Bard!" As I plunged into the five or six Shakespearean sonnets that I knew by heart, Ian looked at me with growing astonishment. God bless him, he started to laugh right there at the altar. When he tried to muffle it, tears streamed from his eyes. Jeanine was not amused. She hissed out several variations of a popular Anglo-Saxon curse that intimated I should have relations with myself. I could have saved Ian a lot of pain if only I'd had a good decongestant.

Across from Jeanine's Kensington Street home I stood watching and waiting. She had done quite well in the divorce and had retained the beautiful terraced townhouse that Ian and she had shared for fourteen months. Quite posh. I stood across the street for six hours, thinking that perhaps I should have "cased the joint" as they say in the films noirs. Gotten a trench coat and made notes on her comings and goings, looking for patterns, that sort of thing. At the very least, worn more comfortable shoes. Just as I was about to give up hope, Jeanine stepped out her front door. Although I had never found her attractive (because of her poisonous personality), I could see that she was still a beautiful woman with a lovely trim figure. She hadn't seemed to have aged at all. Indeed, I have found that to be true with most shallow people. It's almost as if the lack of depth gives the wrinkles nothing to attach themselves to. I followed her.

There were few people on the residential street lined with Georgian terraces, but she was heading for the busiest part of the high street, which would make my job much more difficult. It had to be here, under the shade of the plane trees. I quickened my pace till I was just a few feet behind her. My heart was pounding as I put my hand in my plastic-lined jacket pocket and grabbed a handful of Ian's remains. I raised my hand to the level of Jeanine's reddish coiffure and shouted.

"Jeanine!"

She whipped around, her painted lips pouted in a perfect moue. Before she could recognize me, I flicked a heaping handful of ash smack dab into her deep blue eyes. She reacted as anyone would.

She screamed.

"Ian Becker has passed sentence!" I shouted. I should have left it there but I panicked. "And we're going to need a bigger boat!"

Jeanine actually stopped clawing at her eyes for a moment, trying to make sense of my utterance. The ashes coated her delicate face, and for a moment, she looked like a mime. Feeling more than a little embarrassed at the scene before me, I ran away.

Back home in the safety of my kitchen, I made myself a strong cup of tea. My hands shook as I brought the steaming cup to my lips, but I was exhilarated. It had gone quite well, except, of course, for the *Jaws* reference. I had stayed up quite late last night and caught the last half on Men&Movies channel.

One down, four to go.

WEDNESDAY, SEPTEMBER 12

I did two today without a hitch. The first victim, like Jeanine, was someone with whom I had a personal history. Jeremy Parkinson was the bully who terrorized Ian. He ran the schoolyard with the ruthlessness of a South American dictator. He even had the beard. It has been said that bullies are cowards, and if you stand up to them, they will back down. This was not true of Parkinson. Ian and I stood up to him regularly, and he rewarded our valour with punches, kicks, and repeated dunkings in the girls' loo. Ian once remarked that he had never come across anyone who enjoyed the discomfort of others as much as this yobbo.

Tracking him down was easy, though admittedly not because of my superior detective skills. Our school was having a thirty-five-year reunion and, through an old acquaintance who was on the planning committee, I procured Parkinson's home and work addresses. I went to the work address to carry out Ian's sweet revenge.

Parkinson is the owner of a flower shop near Covent Garden. The only thing that would have surprised me more would have been if he was lead dancer for the London Ballet. He never seemed to have any interest in botany when we were younger, though to be fair, he did favour a willow switch to beat our bare bottoms. Maybe it's strange, but I think of florists as emotional, sensitive types. We never opened our hearts to each other, although I'm sure Parkinson would have loved to have done it literally.

I arrived at the shop just before business hours. I watched as Parkinson opened his door, bringing out green plants and little potted bulbs that he lovingly placed in front of his window. I have to admit that the placement of each flower and plant was quite aesthetically pleasing. Parkinson, not so much. He was about six-three and muscular. He looked like a shaven ape.

I was wondering if he was still the ill-tempered yob that I remembered when he viciously kicked a pigeon hopping near his flowers. I put on my latex glove, stuck my hand in my pocket, and made my way into the store. Parkinson, without looking up at me, said pleasantly, "With you in a moment, sir."

"Take your time," I said, disguising my voice for no good reason. Parkinson would not have recognized it or me. I was chubby last time we met and quite a different-looking person than I am now. Parkinson had his back to me and was fussing with some yellow tulips. I made my way to him, all the while noticing how much bigger he seemed in here with ivy creeping about his shoulders than he did outside. I raised my arm to eye level and cleared my throat. He turned to me, and before he could register what was happening, I flicked. In a voice more panicked and in a higher register than I would have liked, I shouted: "Becker says, 'Kiss my ash!'"

Again, shame coursed through me. It was a vulgar thing to say, and it didn't capture Ian's spirit at all. It was only after I ran away, with the sounds of Parkinson's wounded roar ringing in my ears, that I realized how horrible things would have gone if I'd missed his eyes. As I ran, I stumbled over a disoriented pigeon sprawled on the cobblestones.

In comparison to Parkinson, victim number three was child's play. If child's play involved throwing mortuary ashes. Danny DeLeon was a contractor who had worked on Ian's house. DeLeon had charged a king's ransom for his work, but used shoddy materials and had questionable judgment. He built a beautiful balcony on the second floor that wasn't accessible from inside the house. All the doorknobs were placed on the side of the door closest to the hinges. The door at the back of the house, which led into a lovely English garden, was two feet above the ground, with no stairs to connect it to the landing—that didn't exist. He broke building codes willy-nilly, making Ian's home a dangerous place to live. DeLeon managed to get away with his misdeeds by bribing building inspectors, and he always had an irritating smirk on his face. Today that smirk would disappear. (Danny DeLeon had also worked on my flat. And had overcharged me for a small plumbing job. But that was nothing compared to what he'd put Ian through.)

I surprised him at a construction site while he was sitting in the portable loo. I have to say that this one gave me the most pleasure. I thoroughly enjoyed watching him, writhing and screaming like a little girl, whilst pulling up his knickers as I whispered, "May the Becker be with you!" into his ear.

THURSDAY, SEPTEMBER 13

Almost disaster today! It started off well enough. It was a beautiful bright sunny morning. I had driven quite early to get to the Oxford office of number four: Dr. Kyle Farnsworth. He was a psychologist that Ian had started seeing after his disastrous marriage to Jeanine had terminated. I had never seen my friend in such a fragile state. He had started to doubt his judgment and his talent, and wondered if his life was worth living. His latest Busy

Beaver stories were filled with self-pity and loathing. I'm sure that more than one of his young readers ended up seeking counsel themselves.

Farnsworth was a quack, and his "treatments" set Ian back so much that it took almost three solid years of therapy with a gifted psychologist before he was back to his old self.

To make matters worse, Farnsworth published papers detailing the sessions. He used a pseudonym for Ian, but everyone knew, and Ian was mortified. Farnsworth betrayed Ian's confidence, and exposed his secrets and those of his friends. I looked forward to this "hit." I despise people who take advantage of others when they are at their most vulnerable. Also I'm not fond of the name Kyle.

In addition to his private practice, Farnsworth was a lecturer and course director at the Department of Experimental Psychology at Oxford. The university is quite beautiful and it almost felt wrong to carry out Ian's revenge here. Almost.

Precisely at noon, Farnsworth exited his office and made his way through the hallowed grounds of the university. I quickly gained on my quarry. Just before I reached him, he stopped and fiddled with something in his pocket.

I raised my ash-filled hand and cleared my throat. "Dr. Farnsworth?"

Farnsworth turned around and gazed at me from behind a pair of expensive wraparound Ray-Bans. Damnation! I could throw the ashes anyway, but hitting his Ray-Bans wouldn't fulfill my obligations to my friend. Perhaps if I had Ian's imagination, I could have quickly solved this dilemma. Unfortunately, only one option occurred to me.

"Dr. Farnsworth? Could you take off your glasses for a second, please?"

Looking back, I now realize why Farnsworth didn't feel obliged to honour my request. One: there is no good reason why one should remove one's eyewear when a complete stranger requests it, and two: the chances that the request will be complied with fall dramatically when said stranger has his hand at your eye level, wearing a white latex glove, and is quite obviously holding something.

Farnsworth, of course, didn't remove his sunglasses. He spun on his heels and took off. Actually "took off" is a very generous term. At twenty-five stone, he gently lumbered. I gave chase, but I could have kept pace with him just by walking briskly. He was no match for me, but as it turned out, I needn't have worried anyway. Farnsworth glanced back to see if I was gaining, and ran into a sturdy lamppost. He fell in a heap on his back and his Ray-Bans flew off his face. He lay still for a moment. I thought he might be dead, but after a few seconds, his eyes fluttered open. I released a handful of ash and watched it drift into his eyelashes. Immediately, I felt remorse at fulfilling my friend's wishes. Not because Farnsworth didn't deserve it (he did), but because it didn't seem sporting. It was like stapling a fish to the floor and then placing the fish hook in its mouth. As it turned out, I hadn't time to wallow in my remorse: a number of concerned citizens began to gather and shout angrily at me. I ran.

One to go.

FRIDAY, SEPTEMBER 14

Still shaken from yesterday's adventure, I travelled to Ian's home in Warwickshire to organize his personal effects. I was still trying to track down the last name on Ian's list. Until I did, I could not fulfill Ian's last request.

Connor O'Toole was Ian's most bitter rival. He had actually stolen a few of Ian's ideas and had plagiarized his way to more than a few bestsellers. The courts ruled against Ian in the various lawsuits he had brought against O'Toole, which infuriated him. Ian despised injustice, absolutely abhorred it.

Anyway, as I worked away in Ian's library, I heard a ping come from the computer announcing an incoming email. It was a message from Connor O'Toole!

> Dear Ian,
>
> I must meet with you face to face. I wish to make amends for our past unpleasantness. We can get together either in London or, if you wish, you may come to Kilkenny as my guest. Please consider my request. I will explain all. I await your reply.
>
> Yours,
> Connor

I replied immediately.

> Dear Connor,
>
> I'll meet you in Kilkenny. Arriving on Sunday, September 16.
>
> Yours,
> Ian

I thought it odd that Connor hadn't heard about Ian's passing, but I knew that Connor had become a bit of a recluse since the plagiarism brouhaha. I made the necessary arrangements and packed a bag.

SUNDAY, SEPTEMBER 16

Well, what a day of firsts and lasts! My first trip out of the country, my first time on a plane, and the last name on the list.

The travel part was quite interesting. Going through the security area at the airport, I felt like a sheep shadowed by a particularly grumpy sheepdog. I was flummoxed by having to take my shoes off and completely baffled as to why I was forced to jettison all of the liquid in my carry-on. My imagination is not robust, but could anyone devise a plan that would get them in control of an airplane using their shoes, a Coke, and a can of Barbasol?

As I was led to my first-class seat, I grew excited. I was going to fly! The takeoff was loud and jolting, but I wasn't frightened. The flight itself was delightful. The flight attendants seemed to be disappointed if I refused anything they offered, so I accepted everything. Including a selection of premium beverages. At thirty thousand feet I discovered it was a relief to swallow loudly.

When we landed, the car I had ordered was waiting for me on the tarmac. The driver held aloft a sign with my name on it. The drive to Kilkenny was about an hour and a half, but it went by quickly. The scenery out the window was a picture postcard come to life. I made the driver stop at a pub in one of the small villages on the way and we had a ploughman's lunch, sitting on the benches outside. The patrons, in their lovely accent, regaled each other with tall tales, and there was much laughter. It made me miss Ian even more.

The car dropped me off at the quaint cottage where Connor O'Toole lived. I sent the driver on his way. I did not want him to witness my preparations for the ash toss. I had booked a hotel in town, having decided to take a mini-vacation, and had satisfied myself that it was within walking distance.

I slipped on my glove and rubbed a generous pinch of Ian between my fingers. I knocked twice and waited, hand poised. The door opened, and just as I was about to make my special delivery, the sight before me stopped me in my tracks.

A young man stood in the doorway with his left hand held aloft. He wore latex gloves and he held something grey and powdery.

"You're not Connor O'Toole!" I cried.

"You're not Ian Becker!" he shouted.

In a panic I threw the ashes just he did. Our respective cinders mingled in a cloud of dust and hit us both squarely in the eyes. We reacted as anyone would.

We screamed.

I staggered blindly into the house, knocking the young man off balance. I managed to stop myself from falling by sticking my foot into what I later learned was a nineteenth-century Portuguese cuspidor. I groped about in circles with the thunk-clunk of my steps ringing in my ears.

"Why did you do that?" the young man cried.

My eyes were on fire and my lips were dusted with ash. For a moment, I was reminded of one of my unsuccessful formulas for cats. A high-ash, low-sodium kibble that tasted of crisp bacon. I threw up a little in my mouth. "You did it first!" I hollered.

"Did not!"

"Did too!"

Clearly, this was getting us nowhere fast.

"Enough bickering," I sputtered. "Is there a sink nearby?"

"Yes," said the man. "Follow me."

"That will be difficult. Since I can't see where you are to follow," I said with more than a little sarcasm.

"Don't take that tone of voice with me!"

"I apologize. Can you take me by the hand and lead me?"

"Certainly." He groped for my hand and pulled me to the sink, where we took turns bathing our eyes till we could open them.

Later, over a cup of Irish Breakfast, we compared stories. It turned out Tristram, for that was the young man's name, was a favoured writing pupil of Connor's. When Connor passed recently, in circumstances remarkably similar to Ian's, Tristram was entrusted with the same final request that I had undertaken with such glee.

"My list was quite a bit longer than yours," Tristram said, shaking his head. "Connor had gotten quite bitter in later years. Too bad, really. He was a remarkable man in many ways. Did you know that Ian and Connor were once very close?"

I told him that I was quite surprised to hear it. "That must have been during the time that Ian and I had drifted apart, during to his marriage. I never heard Ian speak fondly of Connor."

"Yes, they were very close, almost like brothers. Then

they had a falling-out. Connor never said why, but I guessed it was over a woman. Few things tend to end a friendship with such rancour."

"I certainly hope it wasn't over Jeanine Carson. That would have been the ultimate tragedy. A friendship broken by that harpy. Did Connor ever mention her?"

"As I said, he never went into it. It's too bad, really. They were so alike in many ways."

"Well, if their choice of revenge is any indication, I would say they were remarkably alike. But given Connor's history, I suspect he plagiarized that idea from Ian too."

"You're lucky Connor's dead. He'd kill you if he heard you say that."

"Tasting his earthly remains is punishment enough, believe me."

Tristram grew thoughtful. "You're right. I've had enough of this revenge business, and if I'm honest, I do understand why Ian would hold a grudge against Connor. There were some marked similarities between Ian's Literal Larry character and Connor's Methodical Man. But the tone of *Literal Larry* was completely different from Connor's story. There was a sweetness to *Literal Larry*. *Methodical Man* was full-blown satire: harsh but very, very funny. Have you read it? It's about a sad chap with no imagination whatsoever."

Realization dawned.

"I think I know why Ian hated Connor," I said slowly. "He was defending *me*. I'm the basis for Literal Larry. When Connor stole Ian's idea, he was making fun of me, and Ian wouldn't have stood for that ..." And then I thought of Ian's list. Every person on it had hurt or cheated me in some way too.

Tristram looked puzzled. "*You're* Literal Larry?"

"Yes, but it doesn't matter anymore." I smiled. I took a last sip of tea. "Well, I suppose that's it, then. It's done. I have to admit I'm glad it has come to an end."

"As am I," said Tristram. "I found the whole thing rather distasteful."

"Ah," I said. "I'm glad for the opposite reason. I was quite enjoying it. Not really something that someone should derive pleasure from, though. So I'm a bit ashamed of myself."

"I wish they could have found peace at the end. Terrible to think that your legacy is so easily undone with an eyecup and a few drops of Visine. It doesn't really change anything."

"I hadn't thought of that, but of course you're right. It doesn't change anything for the dead. But for the living—it might change quite a bit. What are you going to do with the rest of Connor's ashes?"

"There's a bluff near here where Connor and Ian used to discuss story ideas. It overlooks the sea. Connor wanted what was left of him to be scattered to the winds there."

"Hmm. Would you mind if I disposed of the rest of Ian's ashes there too?"

"It has a literary, poetic feeling to it, doesn't it?"

"Yes," I said. "Yes, it does."

Tristram drove us to a spot well off the beaten track. We parked the car and wended our way to the bottom of a wooded valley that opened out onto a crescent moon of sand. The whole beach was banked by majestic rocky cliffs that beautifully accentuated the emerald-green water; it made me feel as if I had walked into a photograph. We went to the edge of the shore and gazed at the blue-green waves that lapped at the sand.

Finally, I spoke: "I'd like to think that, perhaps in death, Ian and Connor can finally reconcile. Find some peace."

"Quite the imagination you have."

I smiled, and on the count of three, we threw the earthly remains of our two friends to the waves. Then we did what sensible people do.

We ducked.

And the ashes blew towards us with the salt wind from the sea.

Faren Heights
Bin 451

INSPIRED BY RAY BRADBURY'S
FAHRENHEIT 451

It was a pleasure to Burn. The whole business of it. From the very beginning of a case when you have nothing but conflicting stories, clues that don't add up, and a cast of characters that wouldn't be out of place in a Hammett novel to the hopefully satisfying conclusion where the story comes together and the bad guys get what bad guys deserve. To Burn McDeere, star employee of the Malloy Detective Agency, solving crime was better than sex. You didn't get as sweaty, and someone else always paid the taxi fare. When the O'Hara case came up, McDeere felt that familiar simmering excitement in the pit of his belly.

Allyson O'Hara had somehow met the impossible challenge of charming his bosses, the Malloy twins. And the founders of the Malloy Detective Agency were harder to charm than an auditor with a migraine. Larry Malloy, the eldest by fifteen seconds, once made a suspect re-enact his own birth by pulling him through the half-open back window of a Nash eight-cylinder coupe. His younger brother, Harry, once went to a doctor complaining of back pain, not realizing he had been shot three times. So when they met with their ace operative, Burn McDeere, and took turns gushing about the aforementioned Mrs. O'Hara, Burn could only surmise that this Allyson woman was one special dame.

"Burn, ya gotta take this case," said Larry. "There's just something about this girl. She's in trouble." He was trying to keep things businesslike, but there was a hint of concern in his bright blue eyes that McDeere almost found touching.

"Yeah, trouble," echoed Harry, running a hand through his sandy hair.

"Boss"—Burn held up his hands in a gesture of helplessness—"I'm kinda swamped right now ..."

"We'll pick up the slack," Larry said, brushing aside Burn's concern. "We've been looking to get more involved than we have been lately. Running a business ain't nearly as much fun as *doing* the business, eh Harry?" Larry winked.

"Yeah, *doing* the business," repeated Harry. Larry was the brains of the operation and was top-notch. Harry was a right guy, but about as sharp as an avocado.

"Okay," Burn said with an exasperated sigh that was more for effect than anything else. "What's the scoop?"

"No idea," Larry said. "She'll only tell *you*. Saw your mug in the paper. A write-up about the San Fran Strangler case. Felt you were the man for the case."

Burn had singlehandedly caught the serial killer who had squeezed the life out of fifteen women, and the arrest had made the front page. The killer was a madman who believed that his victims were alien oranges sent to Earth to take over the citrus drink market. At every crime scene he had left a Valencia with the words "Real Orange" written on the side. Turned out he was the proprietor of an independent juice stand called Real Orange Juice Bar over on Portola. As criminal masterminds go, he had been fairly easy to catch.

"Yeah?" said Burn. "That *was* a good picture of me. Shutterbug got my good side." He offered up his profile: a dark, jutting brow, a flattened nose, and a square jaw. "Maybe she fell in love with my brutish good looks."

"Yeah," said Harry, "and maybe I'm a shoehorn."

Burn and Larry looked at Harry with surprise. This was the first joke Harry had cracked since the stock market crash.

Larry broke the silence. "Listen, she's out there in reception. Talk to her, find out what she needs, and give it to her. Anything you need on this case, you got."

"This broad has really gotten to you, Larry. I didn't realize you were such a bag of mush."

Larry smiled. He picked up McDeere's desk, held it in the air for ten seconds, and put it down gently on the cracked linoleum. "I ain't nobody's weak sister." He walked to the door and turned back to Burn before opening it. "Just take the case. Good money in it, and Mrs. O'Hara ain't too hard on the eyes."

Larry ushered her in.

To say Mrs. O'Hara was not too hard on the eyes was like saying a gunshot to the head stung a little. Not beautiful, no, but very attractive nonetheless, with a quality that made you want to hold her in your arms way past the legal limit. Her chestnut brown hair rested lightly on her shoulders and looked quite happy to be there. Her ocean-blue eyes invited you to take a dip while warning that drowning was likely. Yeah ... she was attractive. A real dish.

"Mrs. O'Hara, this is Burn McDeere, our top operative. He will be more than happy to help you." He gave McDeere a wink and closed the door. Three seconds later he stuck his head back in and whispered loudly, "Harry, you wanna come with me?"

"Sure, sure," Harry said slowly, eyeing Mrs. O'Hara. "Come with you." The Malloy twins left McDeere and Mrs. O'Hara alone in the office.

McDeere shook the delicately gloved hand she offered and gestured to the chair in front of his desk. "Won't you please sit down, Mrs. O'Hara?"

She sat in the chair and slowly crossed her long, slender legs. McDeere kept his eyes on hers and thanked the Lord for blessing him with superb peripheral vision. She tugged suggestively at each gloved finger, then placed her gloves neatly in her lap. Burn stared at them helplessly.

"Would you like a coffee or ... ?"

"I'm fine, thank you, Mr. McDeere."

"Please, call me Burn."

"Unusual name. Were your parents arsonists?"

"Less romantic than that, I'm afraid. Dad just liked the idea of verbs as names."

"Lovely."

"I'm sure my sister Runny wouldn't agree. Cigarette?"

"Why, thank you." She parted her lips slowly and put the cigarette to her mouth in a way that would have gotten her arrested in twenty of the forty-eight states. She held McDeere's hand steady as he offered a light. He hoped she couldn't feel his pulse. His heart was pounding like an over-caffeinated jackrabbit's. She blew out the match and smiled at him. The smoke she exhaled hung between them like a question mark. But there was no question in her eyes. Allyson O'Hara knew exactly what she did to men.

"How can I help you, Mrs. O'Hara?"

"I suppose I should start at the beginning."

"Tends to make it easier to follow."

"I'm very rich. My father owns the Faren Heights Winery in the Napa Valley. You've heard of it?"

"Actually I have. A bit of a fan of the pinot. I know I look like a bourbon guy, but I'm fond of the grape." McDeere did indeed look like a bourbon guy. Strongly built with broad shoulders and an ever-present five o'clock shadow, Burn McDeere was craggily handsome to those who knew what craggily handsome meant.

"Not *excessively* fond, I hope."

"I know my limit ... with wine, anyway."

"Good to know." She smiled. "The winery has always done very well, even during Prohibition. Daddy kept us afloat, I'm sure not always legally."

"Legality doesn't always mean what's right. And it's a God-given right for Americans to get tight on the giggle juice."

"You don't strike me as a religious man, Mr. McDeere. You believe in God?"

"Haven't been able to find him yet. Even with all the clues at my disposal. And I'm a pretty good detective. I try to keep an open mind."

"I certainly hope that's true. Daddy has left the country for a couple of weeks, leaving me to take care of things while he's away."

"Where is he?"

"He's in Argentina chasing down the blue-throated macaw with some friends. Daddy has always loved birds. He is an amateur ophthalmologist."

"Your father helps birds with eye complaints?"

"Isn't that the study of ...? No, wait, I meant entomologist."

"Still off. I think the word you're looking for is ornithologist."

"Say, you're pretty smart." Allyson O'Hara leaned forward slightly, and her eyes shone with interest.

"In some things," Burn replied, leaning back. "Other times, dumb as a bag of hammers."

"Hammers are very useful if you need something nailed." She looked away demurely.

Burn choked on his spit.

"Anyway, as I was saying, I'm in charge right now and I have a little problem."

"Mrs. O'Hara, being the amazing detective that I am, I assumed that you would not be here if everything in your garden was rosy."

She lowered her voice, and leaned forward again. "I need you to find something for me. Something very important."

"What is it you'd like me to find?"

"My car keys."

McDeere looked at her for a long moment. "Your car keys?"

"My car keys," she repeated.

"You want me to find your car keys?"

"I hope you're better at finding things than you are at understanding plain English."

"Why are these car keys so important to you?"

"They start the car."

McDeere couldn't tell whether she was joking. And that, he reasoned, was a quality that could make a woman dangerous. "Is your car missing?"

"No. Just the keys."

"How did you get here?"

"Mr. McDeere, I wouldn't be a very impressive rich person if I had only one car, now, would I?"

"Is there any reason you can think of why someone would take your keys but not your car?"

"I never said someone took my keys. I've misplaced them." She examined her perfectly manicured nails.

"So." McDeere made a temple with his fingers. "You are hiring me to find your keys?"

"I thought I was clear."

"You've just *misplaced* them?"

"Well, yes. It's a big house and I have too many things to look after. I can't waste time looking for something so—trivial. Daddy trusted me to keep everything in order. I would hate to disappoint him."

McDeere shook his head in disbelief. "Mrs. O'Hara, don't take this the wrong way, but I think you're loony."

She looked at him with a smile that was maddening. She opened her purse, took out five crisp one-hundred-dollar bills, and placed them in front of him.

He looked down at the money, then met her glance. "Well, you may be loony, but your Benjamin Franklins make complete sense. All right, Mrs. O'Hara, you have just hired yourself a private detective. May I ask—have you actually *tried* looking for your keys?"

"Oh, yes. A full five minutes. But then I got distracted and stopped. Whenever I look excessively, my eyes get tired and are useless for the rest of the day. I have many things to look at in a day. I need my eyes fresh." Her eyes were a bewitching blue, framed by ridiculously long lashes.

"Yes, of course. Fresh."

"Usually when I return from taking the car out, I hang the keys on a little hook by the door."

"But not this time."

"No, not this time."

"How big is this house of yours?"

"Twenty-two rooms, plus seven bathrooms, a garage that fits five cars, a cabana by the pool, a guest house. And of course the vineyard. Your basic."

"Yeah, basic. That reminds me. I've got to get my Louis XVI armoire rewaxed. And I take it you are not the only one living there?"

"Don't be silly. There's a staff of twelve. Butler, chauffeur, cook, assorted maids, and of course Malaya."

"Malaya?"

"She looks after my son."

"Filipino?"

"No, he's a little white boy. Right now, Daddy's given most of the staff a few weeks off. There's not really a lot to do this time of year. The butler is there right now and a cleaning staff that comes in once a week."

"Must be a hardship. Having to prepare your own meals and such."

Allyson looked at him with a small smile playing at the corners of her lips. "Why, Mr. McDeere. There are things I can do in the kitchen that would make your head spin."

McDeere blinked rapidly three times and tried to recover his power of speech. He fought the urge to shake his head to clear it.

Allyson smiled sweetly. "Oh, would it help if you had a picture of the keys?"

"You have a picture ... of your car keys?"

"I was very much into photography for a little while. Took pictures constantly. Still life was my specialty, although my nudes were quite lovely too." Her gaze fell to the floor as though she were embarrassed, but Burn wasn't buying it. Wouldn't buy it even if she threw in a carton of Lucky Strikes. Allyson rummaged through her purse and brought out a photo. "Here you go."

Burn looked at the picture. The composition was beautiful and the lighting was exquisite. Attached to the key ring, among seven or eight keys, was a small replica of a bird. A falcon.

"What's with the bird?"

"I told you. Daddy likes birds."

"Hmm," said McDeere. "Had a hunch there'd be a better story than that. Feel bad. Usually my hunches are good."

"Nothing interesting about it, really." She jotted a note on a piece of paper. "Here's the address in Napa. Could you be there tomorrow morning at nine?"

"That's fine," Burn replied.

"Just ring the doorbell." She looked deep into his eyes. "You know how to ring a doorbell, don't you? Just push the button till somebody comes."

They sat there looking at each other for an interminable moment. Burn felt every drop of moisture leave his mouth.

This woman had his number and was dialing it hard. "Nine it is," he croaked.

The next day, as McDeere drove his newly washed coal-black Auburn Convertible Cabriolet to the O'Hara house, he was troubled. Nothing about the case seemed right. Why would a wine heiress hire a shamus to find a set of worthless car keys? It could be that his first impression was right: just a dippy dame with too much sugar and way, way too much spice. Even as he thought it, he dismissed it. McDeere had a feeling she wasn't as shallow as she made out. No, that dame was deeper than a Buddhist in a mine shaft. He also knew she wasn't being totally honest with him. It wouldn't be the first time a dame had used the truth like a disposable hankie, but it didn't mean he had to like it. He hated lying and liars. In fact, he was almost a pathological truth teller. Had learned through some bad experiences to tone it down. If you tell the frail who hired you straight out that her man is crushing corsages with a nightclub canary, then suddenly *you're* the one dodging the crockery. Sometimes you've got to soft-soap it a little.

Halfway to the valley, he stopped at a greasy spoon, tossed back a Coke and a fried egg sandwich, and invested a couple of nickels in the phone booth out front.

Twenty minutes later, McDeere pulled up to the address Allyson had given him. Pretty swanky. It was one of those giant mansions that would have looked more at home in the English countryside. Only the acres of grapes that stretched behind the estate distinguished it from your everyday run-of-the-mill castle. McDeere hoped he didn't have to go through the entire house to find the keys. It could take weeks.

He walked up to the door and pushed the doorbell. The door was opened by a man whose face looked like it could chew nails and spit out rust. It was a face that McDeere knew.

"Gurney Malone? When did you get out of the joint?"

"'Bout a year ago. Look, Mr. McDeere, I'm walking the straight and narrow now. I promise you. The best thing that ever happened to me is you putting me away. It changed my life."

Malone had been behind a series of cat burglaries a few years back. He would only hit houses that had cats and would take them along with any valuables he could find. The fixation got him five to eight in Alcatraz.

"Okay, Malone. I believe in second chances. But I would be very disappointed if you were lying to me."

"Nah, don't lie anymore. Takes too much work keeping everything straight. Truth is easier."

I wish that were true, McDeere thought. Sometimes he found the truth anything but easy.

Malone led McDeere into the house. He immediately spied the empty wall hook for the car keys. It was in the shape of a turkey vulture. The first thing you would glance at as you walked through the door. It would be hard to forget to hang your keys there.

The decor was early Audubon. Birds everywhere. Stuffed birds, pictures of birds, statues of birds. The only thing missing were the live ones. McDeere looked at Malone, who shrugged.

"The guy likes birds."

Malone motioned to a room that McDeere surmised was the library. Leather-bound books lined the floor-to-ceiling shelves.

"Mrs. O'Hara will be with you in a minute. You here about the keys?" Malone asked.

"Yeah. Mind if I ask you a few questions?"

"Free country."

"What's the deal with Mrs. O'Hara? Good to work for? As spoiled as she seems?"

"Don't know her that well, really. Her father was the one man who'd hire me when no one was willing to give an ex-con a chance. He's a good egg. She's only been at the house the last couple of weeks. Been in Europe off and on the last ten years." He glanced around to make sure no one was listening. "Rumour is she got knocked up by one of those Riviera playboys and stayed there to hide the scandal from Napa society. I think she only came back to get in the old man's good graces again." He straightened up. "Hey, you know the old man's going to be away for a couple of months with some bird people he knows. He told me they were chasing a blue-throated macaw in Argentina. The rich, huh? They sure are different from us."

"No, they just dress better."

"Anyway, Mrs. O'Hara shows up with the kid, tells us she's here to look after things till Daddy gets back."

"Any way I can talk to Daddy?"

"The old guy's incommunicado."

"No phones in South America?"

"No. He's in the village of Communicado. Somewhere in Argentina."

"Do you know anything about these keys?"

"Only that they're not here. We turned the place upside down. Well, *I* turned it upside down, but no go. The car hasn't been moved since, so it's not like someone wanted to steal it. It's a mystery."

"So if the car is still here, chances are the keys are too. Say, Malone, any cats in the house?"

Malone held up his hands in mock surrender. "No way, boss. Made sure when I applied for the job. Kicked the habit of stealing cats. Been four years pussy free."

"Yeah," said McDeere, "prison'll do that."

Malone glared, then left. McDeere looked around the library. There were a lot of books about birds. A few murder mysteries, a couple of first-edition classics, and a small section on botany. McDeere suddenly wished he had an obsession.

"Mr. McDeere." Allyson entered the library with a small boy following closely behind. "This is my son, Ashley."

McDeere bent down to shake the youngster's hand. "How's it going, Champ?"

Ashley smiled shyly and hid behind his mother's skirts.

"Ashley dear, why don't you go to the playroom while Mother tends to business." She kissed him on the top of the forehead and sent him on his way. She turned to McDeere.

"He's lovely, isn't he?"

"Seems like a nice kid. Kinda ugly, but nice."

"What?"

"Well, you must have noticed. Nothing wrong with being ugly. Builds character."

"Your candour is refreshing. I wish there was a strong man around to influence him. He's very nervous and shy."

"And ugly. Really ugly. No Mr. O'Hara around?"

"No. He was shot in Mexico over a Twinkie dispute."

"Sorry to hear that. There's been a lot of snack-related killings down there recently. Too bad. Mrs. O'Hara, what do you say we get started?"

"Straight to the point. You don't know a lot about women, do you? We like a bit of a lead-up to the main event."

"True, what I know about women wouldn't fill a gnat's navel. I do know that the main event is where all the action is."

She smiled. "The main event it is, then."

McDeere decided the best course of action was to go over the last time she had the keys. They started at the front door, where they were joined by Gurney.

"So. You parked the car, opened the front door. Why didn't you hang the keys on the hook?"

"Gurney had a question for me about my father's office. I got distracted."

"Your father's office?"

"Yes," confirmed Gurney. "Before Mr. O'Hara left for Argentina to search for the blue-throated macaw, he left his office in a horrible state. I wondered if I should clean it up or just leave it."

"Huh." McDeere rubbed his chin. "Why don't we head there?"

They climbed the curved staircase to the second floor, stopping in front of an ornately carved door. They stepped inside. Like the rest of the house, the room was filled with stuffed birds and marble statues of birds perched on pedestals. Papers lay strewn upon every surface.

"Looks like someone was looking for something," said McDeere suspiciously.

"No," said Allyson. "Daddy is just incredibly messy. Most brilliant men are."

McDeere noticed a couple of bottles of wine sitting in the corner. He wandered over and picked one up. The label was a picture of the winery, with a striking font that proclaimed "Faren Heights Bin 451."

"Never heard of this, and I'm a fan of your dad's work. Is it merlot, pinot, cab? Odd that the label wouldn't say."

"Don't know much about this side of the business," said Allyson. "Daddy was always trying new things ... trying to keep the winery at the top of its game."

"Between that and the bird thing, doesn't sound like he had a lot of family time."

"Daddy was who he was."

"Just like Popeye, huh?" Burn smiled.

Just then Allyson's son entered. "Honey," said Allyson, "why aren't you in the playroom?"

Ashley shrugged, then clung to his mother.

Weird kid, thought McDeere. And jeepers was he ugly. Looked like a collapsed lung. McDeere looked around the room and then went over to the large mahogany desk. Upon it was a statue that looked strangely familiar. He'd seen it in a photo. It was an exact replica of the car keys falcon.

"That's odd," said McDeere.

"What?" asked Gurney a little too quickly.

McDeere picked up a small ceramic rhino paperweight. "This doesn't really fit in with the theme of the room. Your father, Mrs. O'Hara, has very peculiar tastes, but there is a pattern. *This* doesn't fit the pattern."

The horn of the rhino had odd grooves on it. McDeere was suddenly slapped with an idea. He picked up the statue of the falcon and turned it around. On the back of the feathered neck was a small opening. The horn of the rhino fit it perfectly. McDeere turned the rhino horn and the head of the falcon sprung open. The statue was hollow, and inside, at the bottom, rested a ring of car keys. Attached was the small replica of a falcon.

"Must have taken a lot of work to misplace your keys in here," said McDeere slowly.

"Took more work to find 'em," said Gurney bitterly.

McDeere spun around. His eyes immediately took in the three guns trained on his head, heart, and groin. The fried egg curdled in his belly.

Ashley, speaking in a voice that was whiskey soaked and high pitched at the same time, chortled, "Thanks for the help, flatfoot."

"A flatfoot is a cop. I'm a shamus."

"Whatever."

"So, you're not an ugly kid after all. You're a dwarf."

"Midget."

"Whatever. And you look like your face got caught in a meat grinder."

Allyson stepped forward. "Sorry it had to be like this, Burn." Her lower lip quivered as though she really meant it. She's good, McDeere thought. Even she believes her lies.

"Throw the keys over," ordered Gurney.

"Gurney, I have to say this is very disappointing. I really thought you had turned over a new leaf. I'm hurt."

"Frankly, McDeere, I don't give a damn. Just throw the keys over."

"Since you asked politely and your gun is pointed at my belly, I guess I'd better." He tossed the keys to Gurney. Gurney caught them one-handed and quickly unscrewed the head of the falcon. A small piece of paper, tightly rolled up, poked out from the body.

"It's here," he called triumphantly to Allyson.

"You mean the research on the super-grape?" McDeere asked innocently.

Gurney scowled. "What do you know about it?"

"Come on, Gurney. I don't just use my head as a place to keep my hat. Something about this case seemed fishy from the start. Asked a few questions of a friend at the Napa Wine Association. First thing I found out is that O'Hara does have a daughter. But she lives in Spain with a painter who draws dogs playing poker. She's still there. Have a friend in the village where she lives. She's quite a famous beauty, apparently. Though she doesn't have the animal magnetism you do, Allyson O'Hara. But that's not your real name, I take it?"

"No," she whispered. "It's Lily."

"You said something about the super-grape," said Gurney, who seemed amused by the ruse. McDeere would have loved to slap him around a little. Gurney had the kind of face that was like a buffet table. You wanted to hit it more than once.

"My friend at the NWA said that there had been rumours flying that O'Hara was developing a super-grape that could grow under any conditions. That would revolutionize the whole wine industry, wouldn't it? I'm guessing that Bin 451 was the first test wine. How is it?"

"It's delightful," said Ashley. "Complex with a meatiness that—"

"Yeah," said Burn. "But O'Hara wasn't going to share it, was he? That would anger a whole lot of people. Especially a small winery trying to make a splash in the industry." McDeere turned to the ugly midget. "A *little* winery situated in Oregon of all places. Lady Littleman Wines. I figure you for the Littleman." McDeere then turned to Allyson. "I guess that makes *you* the lady. Oregon must have a looser definition of the word than we do here."

Allyson's eyes flashed with anger. "We offered O'Hara a tidy sum and"—she paused—"other considerations. He laughed! No one laughs at me."

"Is that why you killed him? For the super-grape or because he didn't want to swim in your lady pool?" McDeere's question dripped with revulsion.

"Don't be disgusting!"

Gurney kept the gun steady. "What makes you think we killed him? He's in—"

"Argentina?" McDeere interrupted. "Chasing the blue-throated macaw? Yeah, you kept pushing that story like it was an old rich lady at the top of the stairs. Only problem is, that particular bird is only found in a small area in Bolivia. And a bird enthusiast like O'Hara would know that." McDeere smiled at the astonished faces of Gurney and Allyson. "Yeah, I've dabbled in birdwatching. If Daddy O'Hara's not in South America, chances are he's dead. I'm guessing buried out back, pushing up the daisies. Be interesting to see if that will influence the taste of the wine."

"Think you're pretty smart, don't you?" Gurney sneered. "Well, you were dumb enough to swallow that straight-and-narrow story earlier. Littleman and I were cellmates on the Rock. Got to be good friends. Told me how his sister was keeping his business going while he was doing time, how they needed a little help. Discovered I had a useful connection. Before I was in for the long stretch, I spent a night in the drunk tank with O'Hara. We'd been at a speakeasy and things had gotten out of hand. He was plastered and kept yapping about this super-grape that was going to make him millions."

McDeere stopped him. "Let me see if I can guess the rest. After you get out, you plead with the guy for a job, which he gives you. A job that gives you access to the whole house. Nice way to repay his kindness. I figure he got wise to you."

"Yeah. So I had to use some *persuasion* to get him to tell me that he had hidden his notes in the little falcon on his key ring." Malone cracked his knuckles (not an easy feat while holding a gun) and shrugged. "He stopped breathing before he could tell me where he hid it. So I told Allyson here to hire you. Knew you could find it and figured that I could get my life back once you did." Malone took a step closer to Burn and raised the gun so that Burn could see down the barrel. "I lost part of my life when you put me away and now I get to take all of your life in return."

"Doesn't seem fair," said McDeere. "My whole life for eight years of yours."

"Well, life ain't fair. So long, sucker."

A shot rang out. Gurney looked down at the hole in his chest, then over to Allyson's smoking gun. His eyes asked a question that would never be answered, then he fell to the floor, dead.

Ashley whipped around. "What the fu—" The bullet ripped through his brain.

"Good shot," McDeere said.

"I just wanted to shoot him in the leg. Misjudged." She shrugged. "Midget."

"So where we at, doll? Didn't want to share the research?"

"No, that's not it at all! I love you, Burn. From the first day we met. Tell me you feel the same," she pleaded.

McDeere looked at her like a kid looks at a car accident. "I usually like to get to know someone before I fall for them. You're a sweet little package, I'll grant you. But I need to know your dreams, your hopes, your fears. I need to find my centre of gravity before I get dizzy with a dame. Call me old-fashioned, but that's the way I roll."

Allyson pointed the gun at him.

"Of course," he said, "I *am* starting to feel *some* affection for you ..."

"You're a fool, Burn! I'm offering you everything! And you dare to turn me down? Me?"

McDeere could see she was going to shoot. He leapt to his left as he pulled his gun from his holster. Her shot almost parted his hair but his found its mark. Shot the gun right out of her hand.

McDeere looked around at the bodies littering the floor. An ex-con, a midget, and a woman holding her hand and whimpering. Make a great beginning to a joke if it wasn't so tragic. Three dead, including old man O'Hara out back. And all because of a stinking grape.

Burn walked over to Allyson and helped her up.

"I could have made you happy, Burn," she sobbed. "Very happy."

"Sure, if I just forgot about the lying and murdering. We coulda been delirious."

"It's not too late, darling." Her eyes were shining bright, too bright for someone who had control of their marbles. "We could start all over. From scratch. I love you. I could make you love me ... I know I could. Could we do it? Could we start a new life?"

McDeere looked at her with a mixture of pity and revulsion.

"Sorry, babe. There will be the beginning of a new way of life. Not for me, but definitely for you."

"Really, Burn? Really?" Whatever sanity remained just took the A train out of town. "When ... when will my new life start?"

Burn smiled sadly and put the handcuffs on her. "When we reach the city, baby. **When we reach the city.**"